The Thistlewood Plot

J. G. Jeffreys

Walker and Company
New York

First published in the United States of America in 1987 by the Walker Publishing Company, Inc.

Published simultaneously in Canada by Thomas Allen & Son Canada, Limited, Markham, Ontario.

Library of Congress Cataloging-in-Publication Data

Jeffreys, J. G.
    The Thistlewood plot.

    I. Title.
PS3560. E45T5   1987   813'.54   87-6100
ISBN 0-8027-5678-6

Printed in the United States of America

10 9 8 7 6 5 4 3 2 1

Editor's Note

IT MIGHT BE unkind to accuse Mr. Sturrock of embroidery but, as he admits in his own postscript, his account differs in some respects from the official versions of the 1820 Conspiracy. There is no record, for instance, of any American involvement; Thistlewood and several others are said to have escaped from the fracas in the loft and were not captured until the following day; the conspirators apparently intended to use cutlasses and bombs rather than the gunpowder which he describes; the actual raid was carried out by a platoon of Coldstream Guards with the police officers. Neither is there any reference to a "Mr. Blake," possibly a Methodist minister, although the bloodthirsty and perhaps insane "Butcher Inge" and his "sack to carry off the heads in" are factual, as is the killing of a Bow Street man in the affray.

Sturrock's account of the intentions of the plot is quite accurate, however. History seems to regard the affair as comparatively unimportant, but in the inflammable situation of 1820 it was certainly quite as dangerous as he claims. Twenty-five conspirators were arrested, and five were transported for life, while five more, including Inge, Thistlewood, and "Orator" Hunt, were publicly executed. Their heads are said to have been held up to the crowd, and there is a macabre note in a later reminiscence of William Makepeace Thackeray, who related how he had heard as a child that the executioner let one of them slip, and was greeted with a howl of, "Yah, butterfingers."

The Dr. Astley Cooper that Sturrock mentions was also a well-known character of the time, and an eccentric man even in an age of eccentrics. It is unlikely that the Royal College of Surgeons would approve of his habits or methods today, but all Sturrock says of him, and more, is recorded in the newspapers and memoirs of the period. He was knighted in 1821 for removing an extraneous growth from King George IV's head; an operation which, understandably, he performed with considerable reluctance.

J.G.J.

=1=

I AM A MAN of kindly disposition and singular patience, whatever my horrible clerk, Master Maggsy, or my sporting coachman, Jagger, may rudely declare to the contrary. Being risen from the humblest beginnings to the chief officer of the Bow Street Police force—of which I have said enough in the past and shall add no more here—I am a person of well-deserved fame but decent modesty, cordially received in the highest society, of a nice gentility with the ladies, and with a well-advised consideration for the nobility and landed gentry. For let a man be as wise as Solomon and as witty as our late poor Dick Sheridan, he is wasting his wit and wisdom on the desert air if he don't find the right people to praise it. In short, one word in the right establishments is worth all of Dr. Johnson's Dictionary in a stable.

Nevertheless, when some humorous rascal sees fit to leave an unwanted, unknown, and damned unwelcome corpse lying at the outer door of my respectable chambers in Soho Square—situated above Mrs. Spilsbury's discreet Dispensary for Marital Disorders, etc.—it calls for wit of another sort. Likewise both kindliness and patience become somewhat constrained. A prank of that kind requests investigation. And to this day my blood runs cold to think of the dread and disaster we'd have had on our hands if I had not set the also aforesaid wisdom to work on the matter.

So to come to the mystery in a few words, the start of it was a tidy little riot at the Tottenham Court end of Oxford Street on a strangely dark late afternoon of February, raining again as it had been raining all that sad and sorrowful winter of 1820, when we were returning from one of Lady Dorothea Hookham-Dashwood's Select Thursday Afternoons at her elegant residence in Hanover Square. Being of a Whiggish disposition— though exceedingly respectable and sensible otherwise— Lady Dorothea would invariably collect an uncommonly mixed menagerie at these curious functions, but seeing that I count her ladyship and her ancient duenna, Miss Harriet, as my most particular friends, I always took care to attend out of politeness. And also out of politeness Master Maggsy and Jagger would be left to wait for me in the harness room or stable, where they were better suited to the company and might not infrequently pick up gossip of a livelier sort.

In the *salon*, however, you might find several of her ladyship's learned pensioners and a Blue Stocking or two prattling about the rights of women and similar fantasticals; or, as the said Dr. Johnson once observed, here a female atheist talks you dead. Very likely you would have an explorer just returned from distant travels, and pretty near always some snuff- and ink-stained Grub Street scribbler looking for patronage. In general, conversation of a most liberal, elevating, and improving kind—if you could put up with it. But I fancy now that on this Thursday our talk somehow seemed to foreshadow the bloody events to come.

There was an American traveller present, by name Mr. Gladwick Mannering; about his early forties I judged, of argumentative manner, but in appearance near enough a gentleman. Suffering the before-mentioned Whiggish persuasions, Lady Dorothea professes a special interest in the members of this New Nation, as she calls it—and so do I for that matter, having enjoyed most cordial relations with several of them over recent years, even receiving pressing invitations to visit when I please—but it was very plain from her sniffs and pecks that Miss Harriet did not much take to this one. And no more did I, for the fellow was talking damned rank republicanism.

'Ma'am,' he was saying earnestly to Lady Dorothea, 'I've been in your country a month or more now and a right pretty country it is. But I've been about in what you call your Midlands and the North, and I'd say that it don't look near so pretty from there. Not with the unrest and unemployment. Being a stranger to your hospitable shores, I'll own maybe that it don't jest become me to say so,' he continued handsomely, 'but I'd say furthermore that your new King George the Fourth ain't near so well loved as he might be.'

'Oh la,' cried one of the Blue Stockings, 'pray don't speak of that great fat *horrid* creature. Daren't show himself in the streets of London for fear his carriage might be stoned. And disporting himself like the Grand Turk in his *ridiculous* pavilion at Brighton. Have you *seen* the latest cartoons?'

'I have,' I said, putting my own little spoke in. 'And damned scurrilous they are. Not to say scabrous. Indeed I'm surprised that any lady of refinement could condescend to look at 'em without feeling a blush rise to her cheek.'

That fetched a blush quick enough, and Lady Dorothea cast a sharpish look at me, but there was no denying that this horse-faced creature and the American were speaking no more than the simple truth.

As he had said, disorder here in London and unsettlement in the North; manufactories going out of business and unemployment rising like the price of bread and everything else. The Jacobin Clubs raising their ugly heads again, and the old King relieved of his sufferings at last, dying mad and blind at Windsor only a few weeks since—and a kindlier gentleman never lived—leaving the Prince Regent to step into his shoes more a figure of derision than a respected Monarch.

There was no denying it, I reflected, while our earnest republican went on with the damned persistence of a carpenter's saw. And I might have known what was coming next. 'There's still talk of the fearful carnage at St. Peter's Fields in your Manchester last August, ma'am,' he announced. 'Even way back in Philadelphia we heard of that. The Peterloo Massacre our newsprints called it.'

'Carnage, tarradiddle, sir,' I retorted roundly. 'Likewise massacre. And if I remember rightly, it was our own *Times* newspaper which first called it that and thundered more than loud enough about it. I'll grant you it was a blunder, and these days a blunder may be worse than a crime. But if you'll pause to hear the truth, it was a crowd of some sixty thousand people addressed by an inflammatory rascal known as Orator Hunt and by no means certain that all of 'em were unarmed and peaceable in intent. Not surprisingly, the Manchester magistrates concluded that the meeting had the appearance of an insurrection, or might easy become one, and ordered the town yeomanry to arrest Hunt. Whereupon fights and rioting broke out, with further inflammatory speeches, and the magistrates next called out the Fifteenth Hussars. God only knows what orders were given or which obeyed, but it seems pretty certain now that the officers were inexperienced and their men nervous, and eleven people were killed and four hundred or more injured. But most of that was caused by the mob itself running wild in panic, and I'll repeat, not all of 'em by any means peaceable or innocent. More than bad enough I'll grant you again, sir, but you'll do no good by harping on it. It was a clear example of human error. Or what may happen when a situation runs out of hand.'

Miss Harriet gave a sniff and peck, but Lady Dorothea spoke with some reproof or as near as she could ever get to it. 'You're somewhat too warm, Mr. Sturrock. You forget that Mr. Mannering is a guest among us.'

'Then I ask his pardon,' I said handsomely, but even so, the man could not leave well alone.

'Why, no, Ma'am,' he answered. 'I'm properly instructed. Yet you'll confess there's call for discontent?' he demanded of me. 'With a stranger's eye here I see two worlds, sir. On one hand I see an extravagence of wealth. It's common knowledge that the play across the gaming tables at White's has never been higher and the rooms at Almack's are thronged night by night with the richest of society. Your clubs, pleasure gardens, and coffeehouses are a crush of elegant fancy. The better quarters of this great city are glittering with gaslights and illuminations and crowded with fine carriages and spirited horseflesh. But what lies in the darker parts, behind the new streets and parks your King George the Fourth and Mr. Nash are designing? I'll tell you, ma'am,' he finished on a solemn hush, 'I'm put much in mind of what our late President Jefferson observed in Paris, when he was ambassador to France at the time of the Revolution.'

'Dear heaven,' squawked another of the pesty Blue Stockings. 'We shall see the guillotine set up in St. James's yet.'

'Damned nonsense,' I said, but then added, 'I ask your pardon, my lady.' Nevertheless, I addressed myself very near as strong to Mr. Mannering. 'Yes, sir, I'll grant you yet again that there's cause for discontent and I speak with a sure knowledge of the labouring classes, which I doubt is more than you do.' I was about to add that I was risen from them myself but thought better of it in present company. 'The most part are decent God-fearing folk, many of the Methodist persuasion,' I continued. 'But they've lost faith in King and Government. And as to whether I blame them or not, I may not say in my position.'

'If I may seem so bold,' Mr. Mannering enquired, 'what is your position, sir?'

'Why, sir,' I replied, 'First Officer of the Bow Street Police Force.'

I fancied he gave me a curious double look on that, seeming somewhat thoughtful for a minute, but I went on, 'The better part also don't like these windy dema-gogues and rabble-rousers any more than we do. Yet there's no doubt that some are turning to confounded dangerous French and American notions.'

'Damned dangerous,' agreed Miss Harriet, with a fresh peck at Mr. Mannering. 'And it's no kindness to encourage 'em. Won't do nobody any good in the end.'

'Quite so,' I said. 'It will not. But what I'm most concerned with, as an officer of the law, is that there's a wicked hell-broth brewing here. And no lack of those who're all too willing to stir it up and ladle it out for empty bellies.'

After that, Lady Dorothea turned the conversation to easier matters, though I noted that Mr. Mannering re-mained strangely silent and thoughtful. But it was not among the best of our Select Thursday Afternoons. Even the Blue Stockings seemed to have a curb on their gabble, and I fancy that all were relieved when Mr. Masters—her ladyship's venerable butler—appeared, to announce that our carriages were waiting.

And also on that, I can perceive my testy publisher rapping on his desk and demanding, 'Be damned, Mr. Sturrock, what is this? I ain't looking for a political dissertation after the fashion of that feller Cobbett. If that's what I wanted, I could find a score of hacks who'd do it better at a ha'penny a line. You promised us a diverting entertainment for the ladies, to start with a corpse left untidy on your doorstep. So where the devil is it?'

To which I shall reply, 'Why sir, we're coming to our corpse fast enough. We're coming to a plentitude of corpses, not to speak of a most diabolical conspiracy. But you must needs lay out the table before you can sit down to your supper.'

One way and another I was not in the best of tempers as we turned out of Hanover Square in my new chaise—an elegant little turnout purchased at vast expense, delivered only a month before from the coach builders. It was in a thickening drizzle of rain, more than a touch of fog, already very near as dark as a sow's belly, and I told Jagger, 'Keep it brisk but steady. And I'll have your guts if you so much as scratch my paintwork,' I added, for there was a fair confusion of traffic at the better end of Oxford Street—even worse than common with the rattle and clatter of hoofs and wheels, horses steaming in the damp, the bob and flicker of lamps, and sundry observations and curses from the ruder sort of drivers.

There was further trouble to come as we passed the new Regent Street. First, many of the shops had their lights doused and shutters put up, and half-seen gangs were jostling in the dark. Here a tradesman's van left unattended, there a costermonger's barrow overturned and urchins fighting for what was left of its contents. At one corner tavern a lurid flicker of torches, and an unkempt villain haranguing the crowd and brandishing a ragged Tricolor: a sight I never thought to see in London. Then a drunken and disorderly rabble howling that horrid doggerel, 'When Adam delved and Eve span, who was then the gentleman?' and milling all over the road ahead of us.

It was a spectacle to frighten our horse, and the resourceful Jagger did not wait for orders but pulled in sharp some distance short of the mêlée. 'So what's to do?' he demanded. 'We'll get more'n our paint scratched if we try to whip through that lot.' While Maggsy announced, 'My oath we shall. They'll have us arse over tip and scrag us.'

'Quite so,' I agreed, as a fresh rout of urchins started to make free with clods of dung and other undesirable missiles. 'Give 'em the lash, Jaggs,' Maggsy bawled, punching one importunate rascal on the nose, and for once even I thought it best to let valour wait on discretion. We were then only a little way beyond an opening on the right, and I said, 'The rain'll soon cool these scoundrels' high spirits. None of 'em likes water, however applied. Turn back and pull off down Chapel Street. We'll come into Soho Square the back way.'

Had I but known it, that was a momentous decision, but there was little chance for such reflections then, for even as Jagger pulled us round to cross the road, a town phaeton somehow broke out of the confusion ahead and came roaring down on us hell for lick, damned near taking our horses' noses off. There was a scatter of the rabble chasing and howling behind it and a Dandy driving one-handed, lashing his whip about with the other, hallooing like a madman for way, and gone in a flash, though for one brief instant I caught a glimpse of a woman's face gazing at me as the carriage careered past. By now, however, Jagger had us on somewhat less than one wheel, and there was neither time nor breath for civilities, apart from various observations. I fancy also that several of the savage villains about us were considerably discommoded, but God only knows how we got round safely into the narrows of Chapel Street.

Once there, in darkness and quiet and on an even keel again, I expressed myself with some freedom, but Maggsy said, 'Better'n being gutted if them frolicsome little lambs'd catched us.' He peered out to look where we were, observed, 'Nobody much about here anyway,' and then asked, 'Did you note a young woman in that other kerridge? Seemed she was looking as if she might know you.'

'Then she didn't stay long enough to pass the time of day,' I replied shortly. 'Can't hardly blame her, can you?' he enquired, and there the matter ended, for by this time we were turning thankfully into our own territory. You could still hear the grumble of the mob and perceive an uneasy flicker above the buildings on the north side of the square by Soho Street, but otherwise all appeared silent and dark here save for a few upper windows and fanlights casting a misty glow into the thickening fog and rain. There seemed to be the movement of a brief, furtive shadow by our area railings, but I saw nothing more amiss at first, except that the bracket lamp above our door was not yet lit, as it should have been by now. Neither was there any light in Mrs. Spilsbury's consulting or reception rooms, and Maggsy remarked, 'So she's out or gone away, and Grommet's on the gin again.' This Grommet being the good lady's doorkeeper, who resided in the basement.

So we discovered our corpse, or to be more precise, Maggsy damned near fell over it. When we alighted, Jagger took the chaise on quick to the mews without a second look, being concerned about his horses. Maggsy scurried across the pavement just as fast to open our door, while I paused an instant to peer across the square for I had heard, or I thought I had heard, a sound that means no good to anybody: the sharp click of a pistol being cocked. I thought also that I could make out another furtive movement in the middle space where carriages wait, one or several thicker shadows, but it was too confounded dark to be sure of them, and before I could issue a challenge, Maggsy's melodious voice rent the silence. 'God's whiskers,' he screeched, 'What's this, then?'

I turned about fast after the wretch, demanding, 'What's what?' then reflected briefly that only Maggsy could ask a damnfool question like that, for what it was appeared all too plain even in the dark, sprawling face down between the pillars at the top of our steps. At first sight I fancied the fellow was merely drunk and was about to reprimand him severely before I perceived that there was something far more amiss with him than liquor. 'Get that door open quick, and let's have some light,' I commanded Maggsy, bending closer and now discovering a warm and wet patch on his back, low down to the left side. 'Come, my man, what's happened to you?' I asked kindly, while Maggsy scrambled over us and fumbled with his key.

I was rewarded by the faintest suspiration of breath, half between a groan and a bubbling sigh, seemingly uttered into the doorstep. 'Stabbed in the back, you fool,' the fellow whispered. 'If you're Sturrock you're too damned late.'

I heard Maggsy fling the door back with a crash, cursing inside in the dark, and I asked, 'Looking for me, were you? Well, you've found me right enough, and you're in good hands now. God's sake, get a light,' I repeated to Maggsy.

The man made a further sound like an ill-tempered expiring laugh, though it was all I could do to hear it. 'Too damned late by five minutes,' he muttered, and then seemed to gather up the rest of his strength. 'Listen,' he got out. '*Delenda est Carthago* . . . Cato . . .'

He tried to add another word, but his voice died again and I thought he had gone. 'Come now,' I urged him, 'try again,' and he said suddenly and clearly, 'Ask what time does the . . . ' but then coughed and choked.

And on that, everything happened at once. Maggsy at last struck a light, which seemed like a sudden blaze of hellfire in the darkness. It revealed our corpse, with its face staring sideways in a horrid, grinning rictus, and illuminated Maggsy gazing pop-eyed past me across the square. Then my wretched man let out another dreadful screech and fell on me, thrusting me down with him and at the same instant there was a brighter flash, the bang of a pistol, and a ball which came slamming past my head. 'Be damned,' I observed in some surprise.

'You bloody will be if you stop here much longer,' Maggsy screamed. 'Inside,' he bawled as a second pistol crashed, this time the shot coming wicked close to my left ear, so damnation close that I did not pause for further discussion, but bundled Maggsy inside, got in behind him, and slammed the door after us, all uncommon fast. 'Be damned,' I said again in reasonable vexation. 'What is this?'

'What's it look like?' Maggsy snarled. 'Somebody waiting for you. And not all that loving disposed neither.'

'Then they won't have to wait long,' I announced, thrusting past him to get up the stairs to our chambers to fetch my own weapons. 'What the devil is London coming to?' I demanded. 'Shooting at a man on his own doorstep. If that's the sort of match some rascal wants, he can have it.'

Nevertheless it was a vain hope, as I perceived for myself without Master Maggsy's rude advice. The villains were hardly likely to linger for any further compliments. They would be away and lost in the mist and the short streets beyond the square before I could have my own weapons primed. Moreover, there was the necessity of lighting a lamp to do it, and before that I must needs spare time to take an observation through our sitting room window in the dark. Altogether five precious minutes lost.

But in the brief survey I allowed myself, I could see some sort of movement down below. There were several uncertain figures flitting about close by our porch, though what the devil they were doing I could not make out, and I did not linger too long watching them. My first thought was that so far from making themselves scarce, the rascals were actually proposing to add insolence to impudence by invading us, and I was quick about pulling the curtains across and charging my pistols. I half expected to hear the noise of battle from below at any minute, and I was resolved to reply with a hellish hot reception.

All remained strangely quiet however, even Master Maggsy. By the time I came down the stairs again, he had got the lamps lit and was standing well back from the door whispering to Mrs. Spilsbury's fellow, the aforesaid useless Grommet, in a loud aroma of gin. 'God's sake,' that fart-wit cried, squealing like a winded pig at the sight of my armament, 'what's all this shooting and banging, Mr. Sturrock? I hope you ain't starting to bring your work home with you. Mrs. Spilsbury nor her clients won't like it.'

'Confound Mrs. Spilsbury,' I retorted, 'with the greatest respect. And confound you. Take your goose face out of this. Has there been any further movement?' I asked Maggsy.

'Don't know, and don't mean to look, neither,' he answered rudely. 'Seemed like a kind of whispering and scuffling a bit since, but can't hear nothing now.' He also gazed at my pistols fearfully. 'You ain't going out there, are you?'

'Not precisely,' I answered, deciding on a better tactic. 'I'm going to invite the villains in.'

'You're *what?*' he demanded, but I took up my position behind the corner of a tall armoire, whence I could derive a certain protection yet still command the door, and said, 'Now then, when I give the nod, pull it open sharp and keep behind it.'

'You can be damnation certain I'll keep behind it,' he assured me fervently. 'D'you know what you're doing?'

'I've a fair notion. I want to know what's afoot here, and I mean to wing a brace of the rascals at least to find out. And you'll be best out of the way, my man,' I advised Grommet. 'You're no hero, and there'll be bullets flying in a minute.' That admirable worthy let out a fresh squeal of terror and vanished down his basement steps like a rabbit—very near fell down by the sound of it—and I added humorously to Master Maggsy, 'If there's more than a hundred of our birds you may take 'em in the rear.'

He replied with something remarkable profane but went to his place, and I cocked my Wogdens. 'Now!' I announced, and Maggsy uttered a short prayer. He snatched back the bolts, heaved back the door with a crash, and made himself as small as he could.

And our sporting coachman had the nearest escape of his life.

It is a mercy that I am as steady to hold my fire as I am to shoot, or at that instant Jagger would have been shorter by a head. He came plodding in like an idiot drayman with his fearful horse grin, announced cheerfully, 'Proper pissing down with rain now, and the fog's as thick as Mother McGinty's soup,' But I never saw a grin vanish quicker. 'Godamighty,' he cried, 'what're you doing? Don't point them things at me. What've I done?'

'Nothing, but very near got your eyebrows blowed off,' replied Maggsy, emerging from his hiding place, while I took a minute to get my breath back before demanding, 'If it comes to that, what the devil are *you* doing? Did you not see that fellow on the doorstep?'

'Ain't nobody on the doorstep,' Jagger said, gazing at me strangely. 'Has he been took curious?' he asked Maggsy.

'No more'n usual,' Maggsy snarled, but feeling my breath come short I thrust them both aside to get to the door and see for myself, though by now I had little doubt of what I should find—or what I should not find.

Jagger's wits might not be all that wonderful, except when it came to horseflesh, but he was near enough human to have a pair of eyes in his head. So I was not surprised, yet at the same time dumbfounded speechless. For, as he had said, there was nothing there. Or nothing save an ugly dark patch already running off into rivulets in the unrelenting rain. And also, now revealed in the light from the hall, one small object lodged against the foot of the area railings.

For what little that might be worth I took it up, discovering a soft leather pouch or wallet of some sort, and then paused for another minute to look about. But the fog was now so thick that you could not have seen a haystack at five paces, while the silence was broken only by querulous enquiries somewhere, an upper-floor window slamming down, and Maggsy demanding fearfully, 'God's sake come in, will you, and let's have this door shut again.'

'So there we have it,' I announced, when the situation calmed itself somewhat and we were in conclave in our sitting room. 'The entire profit of the affair, for all it may tell us. One mere tobacco pouch and a handful of tobacco.'

'It's an uncommon good'n though,' Jagger observed, taking it up from the table to examine it. 'Best Morocco leather and oil silk lining. The tobacco's hardly got damp.'

'So I perceive,' I agreed. 'From which we may infer

that it had not been lying out for long. But we'll come to that in a minute. First of all, did you see or hear anything in the square as you came through? Had you but known it, you took a fearful risk, coming round by the front.'

'My oath, I know,' he cried. 'Seeing you with them damned quick pistols of yours on me. I ain't likely never to forget it. The back door was locked, so I concluded Grommet was on the bottle again.'

I was a trifle testy with him. 'You were in danger from the villains who carried that fellow away. It's plain they don't stand on ceremony, and they'd very likely've done for you as well. You must've missed 'em by inches. But did you *see* anything?'

The good simple fellow scratched his head. 'Never a thing. You couldn't see an Irishman's donkey out there. I fancy there was two or three upstairs windows open somewhere, as somebody was demanding what the hell was going on. Likewise I heard a kerridge of some sort going out of the square by way of Sutton Street.' He pondered over that for another minute. 'Come to think of it, that might've been a tradesman's van. It'd got that sort of rattle about it. And one horse. Which same was going a bit dab-footed, as if it had a shoe working loose.'

Maggsy sniffed evilly. 'And that's a wonderful lot of use.' He turned his horrible gaze on me. 'Nor I don't suppose you had the chance to see much of this cove, neither.'

I shook my head. 'I did not. I've a notion of a rough frieze jacket and gaiters, as if he might have been a stablehand or groom, but little more. Yet it's an uncommon groom who speaks Latin. "Cato . . . " he said. "*Delenda est Carthago* . . . " Which in the vulgar tongue means, "Carthage must be destroyed." But what the devil a disagreeable old Roman and Carthage may have to do with anything that concerns me God only knows. Likewise his last words. "Ask what time does the . . . "

It's plain he was bringing a message of some sort, but could only get that much out. Confound it, if we'd only come straight into the square we might've caught him in time. That few minutes made all the difference.'

'Made a difference to us as well,' Maggsy observed, 'if you fancied being scragged.' He turned his wicked eye on Jagger, who had now filled his pipe from the pouch and was savouring the tobacco. 'What's it like, Jaggs?'

Jagger puffed out a singularly rich and aromatic cloud. It seemed high-flavoured and not much to my taste, as I prefer a simple Latakia, but our sporting coachman pronounced, 'My eye.' He considered it for a few more whiffs and then added, 'That's a bit of the proper. It's an uncommon stablehand who speaks Latin, says you. And I say it's a partic'lar uncommon who smokes bacca like this. Nor he didn't get it for tuppence an ounce, neither.'

'So ho,' I said, taking the pouch to examine it myself, perceiving that it was a coarse-cut leaf of a reddish colour and a trifle sticky to the touch. 'As you so profoundly observe, Jagger, it's out of the ordinary. And indeed a most uncommon stablehand. So we begin to discover something about him after all. And tomorrow you and Maggsy shall set out to discover something more. I'll have you go to Mr. Tomlin's tobacco and snuff shop in Charing Cross to ask him what this is, and if he supplies it to any customers. If he does I want their names.'

'Asking a lot, ain't it?' Maggsy objected, true to his contumacious nature. 'Tomlin's ain't the only tobacco shop. There's any number of 'em.'

'To be sure, there are,' I agreed. 'And you may try them all if you must. But Tomlin makes a boast of rare tobaccos, and he's the best to start with.'

So thus simply did we set to work to unravel a most damnable affair, which but for me might have let all hell break loose in London.

=== 2 ===

TOMORROW BROUGHT ITS own vexations, and one in
particular that still makes my breath come short when I
think about it. The day started quiet enough, though
remaining foggy. Having dispatched Maggsy and Jagger
about their enquiries, I betook myself to the St. Giles
Mortuary which is close behind old St. Giles's Church
and a gloomy edifice, as all such melancholy receptuaries
are. Commonly they are managed by custodians just as
melancholic, but the keeper here was a notable exception
to the rule, being an unseasonably cheerful fellow. A
curiosity altogether, indeed. Appropriately named Jonah
Gotobed and little more than half a man; he had only a
left eye and a right leg, having mislaid the other members
at the Battle of Trafalgar with Lord Nelson. There he
had served as a Loblolly man, or Surgeon's Mate, a
calling which had endowed him with certain anatomical
experience and a nice professional interest in his clients.

'Why now, Mr. Sturrock,' he cried, stumping on his
one leg, 'here's a pleasure and privilege to brighten the
day. And what might I do for you this time? Is it one of
my clients you're looking for?'

'It might be,' I said. To tell the truth I had little hope of
it, but this comical little fellow frequently heard more
than he liked to confess concerning the sundry mysteries
and unholy doings in our Parish of St. Giles. 'I'm seeking
a fellow who had an unfortunate accident with a knife

yesterday. It's not all that likely, but he might have been left lying about in one of the courts or alleys somewhere.'

'And so come home to roost here?' Jonah pursed up his lips and shook his head. 'I'm feared not, Mr. Sturrock. I like to oblige if I can, as you well know. But I don't have nothing of that sort to hand so far. An accident or two, to be sure—the fog brings 'em on. But not what you might call a hunfortunate accident. With a knife, did you say?'

'Or some such implement. Well enough then. It was a forlorn hope at best. Nevertheless, a whisper from you wtih some of the hospital anatomy-room porters might not be wasted. Or a quiet word with some of the Resurrection Men.'

The rascal knew what I meant well enough and gave me a sideways look out of his single eye. 'Steady as you go now, Mr. Sturrock,' he protested. 'Haul on your braces, sir. I don't have no truck with them gentry—not in my position of trust. Nor the anatomy rooms don't accept accidents of that sort, neither.'

'Not officially they don't, and very right and proper.' I gave him my hanging-judge smile. 'But a corpse found is easier money than a corpse dug up, and there's many a telescope clapped to a blind eye. In short, Jonah, I want information and I mean to have it. Moreoever, there might be a sovereign looking for a good home if I get it quick enough.'

He shook his head again. 'Quick or slow, it ain't so easy. It'd be a privilege to oblige, Mr. Sturrock. It's a Ship's Regulation with me—oblige the Law and your proper officers, whatever else you might do. All the same, hunfortunate accidents is best left well alone unless they're delivered here in ship-shape order and entered in the Day Book. To be plain with you, sir, I don't know.'

'Jonah,' I advised him kindly, 'reflect on a famous observation by Dr. Samuel Johnson. Begod, he made so many that I wonder he ever found time to do anything else. Knowledge is of two kinds, he observed. We know a subject ourselves, or we know where we may find information on it. And I want such information about this unhappy fellow, whatever it might be. Pretty well anything will merit praise for devotion to duty in the right quarters.'

He gave me another sideways look. 'It takes a lot of praise to mend a cut throat. But did I fancy you spoke of a sovereign?'

'I might have done,' I said. 'It might bear thinking of.'

So having thus cast a bait at random, I left our one-legged Charon still shaking his head after me and turned my steps next through the fog to the Bow Street Office.

As to what awaited me there, it were better to set it down in terms as polite as I can. There was a stink in the air to start with, and no sooner had I appeared, barely drawing off my gloves, then old Abel Makepenny stuck his quill pen halfway up his nose—a curious affectation he suffers in times of agitation—and announced, 'Lord God Almighty wants you instanter. He's been bawling to know where the devil you are this last hour or more.'

This Abel being our ancient Chief Clerk, and Lord God Almighty not precisely what he might sound, but merely the First Magistrate. Abel now so elderly and full of knowledge that he would make Methuselah seem a beardless boy, and the other only lately appointed and still fresh to our ways; thus somewhat inclined to rise a bit above himself when he got the chance—though a very tolerable gentleman now and again. In brief, he had not yet got so far as to perceive that me and Abel were generally used to arranging everything very nicely between ourselves. But we were in hopes of teaching him better before he got much older, and I said, 'Compose yourself, Abel. I'll calm him.'

But that was a boast easier to promise than to perform. When I entered Mr. G's sanctum, he greeted me much the same as Jonah Gotobed, though with a very different intent. 'Well here's a privilege, Sturrock. It's devilish civil of you to condescend to wait on us now and again.'

He was in his sarcastic mood, I noted, resolving to give him as good as I got. 'Why, sir, that's the second time today I've been so welcomed. The first occasion was by the keeper of the St. Giles Mortuary.'

He contrived somehow to blink with surprise and glower at the same time. 'The St. Giles Mortuary? What in damnation was you doing there?'

'A matter of murder, sir. As you may know, it's a misdemeanor that we're inclined to disapprove of here.' But it was advisable to use a nice diplomacy. It might smack of carelessness to admit to discovering a corpse on my doorstep and then allowing it to elude me. 'Proceeding on certain indications brought to my attention, the affair struck me as having undesirable peculiarities. It arose following a visit to take tea with Lady Dorothea Hookham-Dashwood at her residence in Hanover Square.'

As all the ladies will know, the truth is a precious jewel so long as you don't tell too much and mix the rest up a bit. By so delicately putting it that it seemed as if the nobility and gentry were concerned with a murder should have brought Mr. G. to attention on the instant, for he dearly loved a fine title. But this time he forgot himself and his proper manners.

'Mr. Sturrock,' said he, with great deliberation. 'You are a jumped-up jackass. Furthermore, I have heard you called a puffed-up bullfrog and by God, I believe it. Moreover, you have an insufferable conceit of yourself. And you allow yourself airs above your position to boast so free of your high-placed friends.'

It was very clear that the good gentleman was afflicted

with considerably more than last night's port or something that had disagreed with him at breakfast, but I was resolved to keep the conversation as genteel as I could. 'Sir,' I said, 'I hope I may choose my own friends, but I am not so fortunate with my professional company. That is thrust upon me.' For a minute I was afraid he might be taken with a stroke, but I asked, 'Nevertheless, might I enquire why you see fit to compliment me so warmly this morning?'

'You might,' he announced when he had recovered his breath. 'You might, indeed. Have you seen *The Times* newspaper today?'

He did not wait for me to answer—and as it happened I had not, since I prefer to read it at the office at somebody else's expense—but snatched the paper up from his desk to read from it. " 'A disgraceful fracas in Oxford Street last night", ' he declaimed. 'And a leader, Mr. Sturrock. Listen to this. "We have said before, and shall doubtless say again, that the labouring classes have cause enough, and more than cause, for their present discontents. But that is not to say that these very proper grievances can be alleviated by this or similar scenes of violence and destruction." '

He paused to get another breath and then continued, ' "We do not ask for miracles of Lord Liverpool's so-called Administration but we are entitled to ask why the noble lord's Government is doing nothing, either to ameliorate these discontents on one hand, or to stem the rising tide of dangerous Radicalism on the other . . ." There's a piece more in that vein,' he finished. 'But here's the nub that concerns us, sir. "Above all we are entitled to ask why no attempt was made to quell this disturbance, or at the least to arrest its ringleaders." So what do you make of that, Mr. Sturrock?' he enquired.

I answered him in the reasonable tone of a man wondering what in damnation all the pother was about.

21

'It's the Old Thunderer giving tongue again, and as usual telling us all what we already know. Or you might say that they're asking for another St. Peter's Fields—which they'd be the last to appreciate if they got it. But otherwise I don't see why it should concern us.'

'Don't you, by God?' There was a brief strange silence, like the evil calm that sailors say lies at the heart of the most dreadful storms, and then he thrust another paper at me. 'So maybe you'll be good enough to tell me what you see in that.'

It was a letter. Written on a good sort of paper, from an excellent address—54 Portman Square—in a firm, clear hand. There was no untutored maidservant or denizen of the Seven Dials here. It was superscribed, 'To the Chief Magistrate, Bow Street Police Office,' and it was started, 'Sir: I wish to lodge a complaint of cowardly and gross disinclination towards duty against one certain of your *first officers* . . . '

'Well I'm damned,' I observed, for it continued, 'I was in a carriage at the lower end of Oxford Street last evening when our conveyance was impeded and set upon by an *inflamed and unruly mob*, with missiles and insults, etc. Had it not been for the extreme gallantry of my driver, we might well have been overturned at the cost of our lives, or *worse*. I then perceived *your officer* some safe distance off, sitting composed in his own carriage and surveying the riot. I had thought he was present with intention to *Impose the Authority of the Law*, but what a vain hope that proved. For seemingly having no consideration but for his own safety, he plainly caused his own driver to turn about, and *so fled the improper scene in unmanly haste* . . .'

I paused to take a deep breath myself, and Mr. G. said, 'God help us if *The Times* gets ahold of that. Read the rest of it, Sturrock. Don't put yourself out. Read it slow and careful.'

Slow and careful be damned, for it was more than plain enough. 'I require you to reprimand this officer *in the severest possible terms*, and I further inform you that I am strongly advised, by *a very influential person*, to bring this matter to the *notice of Higher Authorities* and the public newsprints. I am, sir, yr obdnt svnt, Julia Bracegirdle.'

'Well,' asked Mr. G., 'What d'you say to that?'

'Malice, sir,' I replied. 'Malice naked and unadorned. And more behind it, unless I'm much mistaken. Who the devil is this Julia Bracegirdle?'

'I don't know, and I'm damned if I care,' he roared. 'Godammit, you don't deny it was you? You're the only one of my men who has the face to boast his own carriage and coachman.'

I felt my neckcloth growing dangerously tight, but restrained myself. 'Sir,' I said, 'the manner in which I choose to live is my own business.'

It was clear by now, however, that the man was determined to pick a quarrel. 'Not when it's disinclination to duty and fleeing the scene in unmanly haste.'

'And pray, sir, what would you have had me do?' I enquired. 'Dismount from my chaise to hold up my hand and cry "Desist"? If so, I shall beg leave to advise you that you are not yet familiar with the playful habit of the London mobs.'

'Afraid of 'em were you?' he demanded spitefully. 'Careful of your own skin?'

Now nobody calls me afraid without grave risk to himself. Nonetheless, I was still determined on a proper politeness. 'Sir,' I said, 'I fear nothing human. But I'll confess to some trepidation when dealing with a jumped-up jackanape dressed in a little brief authority.'

It was clear that the discussion could not continue much longer, for he seemed to take that somewhat personal. 'By God . . . ' he got out, and I waited with interest for what might come next. And when it came it was exceedingly plain and simple. 'Sturrock,' he pronounced after several remarkable embellishments, and in a whisper that was meant to come out as a roar, 'you're relieved of your duties forthwith. From this very instant.'

It took even me a minute or so to digest that. I was struck incredulous by the folly and impudence of it, but concluded that the poor distracted man did not realise what he was doing. Then, however, I answered just as simple. 'Very good, sir. Pray permit me to observe that I am indeed relieved—and I hope you may not regret the relief before I do.'

With that final courtesy I took my leave, very near bowling over Abel Makepenny on my way out. The excellent old gentleman was already well informed, having been listening at the door in the outer office, and I shall not repeat even the least of his observations; but I was surprised that he also enjoyed such a wide command of our descriptive English language. And when he had exhausted his vocabulary, we made certain private arrangements of our own.

Even Abel's fulsome poetics were pale to Master Maggsy's when we met in The Brown Bear and I informed him of my late surprising promotion. 'You're *what?*' he demanded incredulously. He stared at me with his eyeballs very near dropping out on his cheeks and then plunged into such an extravaganza that in the end I was obliged to cut him short. There were always interested parties in The Bear, and the news would get about fast enough without having it announced by a Town Crier.

'Have done,' I told him testily. 'It'll be all over Drury Lane by tonight without you making an opera of it. I'm not all that concerned except for the insult. It's a positive privilege to be discharged by a jumped-up Jack in Office who ain't yet discovered his arse from his elbow. Within a week he'll be down on his knees imploring me to go back, and by God I'll see that he chews on a tasty bit of crackling then. We shall do well enough. The pittance I draw from Bow Street don't barely keep our horses in fodder, and I've already got plans of my own. And the first of 'em,' I added, 'is to find out who and what this damned Julia Bracegirdle might be. I've a bone or two to pick with that lady if she exists. And I've more than a notion that if she does, she and the fellow on our doorstep last night might not be so far apart.'

'Did you tell 'em about that at the Office?' Maggsy asked.

I called for my usual pot of claret to compose myself. 'I did not. I didn't get the chance. And now it's a particular special and private corpse that I mean to keep all for ourselves. So let's have your report first. What did you glean from the tobacco shops?' I noted then that our sporting coachman was nowhere to be seen. 'And where's Jagger?'

Maggsy was still muttering darkly into his beer, and he shook his head. 'God knows. Gone to look for a noise he thought he heard, like the man in the play. If you ask me, this is a right rum go all round. I'll tell you in a minute. But just you have a look at that cove across there to start with. D'you know who he is?'

I cast a glance across the taproom, not with much interest. It seemed to be the common company here, most fair-to-middling rascals, though somewhat improved since the late landlord, Wall-Eyed Jack, got himself taken off from a shortage of blood after an unfortunate discussion with a pair of sailors some months since. Otherwise there was only one stranger: a smallish fellow with a foxy eye, and all the cunning air of the old soldier about him; decently enough dressed yet not at ease in his clothes, and a face squinting at us sideways over his pot, and there was a cut about him that recalled something to me, if I could have bothered to think what it was. But I had no time for diversions then, and I said so, short and plain.

'You don't recollect him then?' Maggsy asked. 'Thought you never forgot a face? You'll know him in a minute though. I'll lay a penny to a pinch of snuff that he'll be over here before long. He's had one eye on me ever since I come in, and he's been listening to every word we've said with both ears wagging. I reckon he's been waiting for you.'

'Then he can wait a bit longer,' I said. 'Let's have your report.'

'Have it your own way.' The wretch took a draught from his tankard and then nodded mysteriously. 'And as to that, the plot curdles. We took that bacca to Tomlin's shop not expecting much of it, but as it happened we was lucky first go. Old Tomlin was a bit suspectious to start with, as I fancy Jaggs must've been saucy with him some time of late, but he took a look at the bacca all the same, and then announces that it's in very small supply on partic'lar order, and not by no means in our common class. That bacca, he says, is a fine, rare old Kentucky burley, cured in rum and molasses; he don't know of more'n three gentlemen who smokes it. One being at the American Embassy, who gets his own sent over private, the other two being customers of Tomlin's, who he procures this aforesaid small supply for special.'

'So ho,' I said. 'We make progress. So you had their names?'

Maggsy scowled balefully. 'We did not. And not my fault neither. That was Jagger's doing. You know Jaggs fancies his wits a bit sometimes, and he must need open his big mouth. He says, 'Very good, Mr. Tomlin, we'll have all the information about 'em if you please, and this is Bow Street business".'

'Dear God,' I observed. 'I'll have that rascal's guts. Where is he now? And what did Tomlin say?'

'I'd as soon not repeat it, but it was uncomplimentary. The least was to so and so ourselves off, and he didn't give no information about his customers to nobody. And as to where Jaggs is now, or might be if he ain't got his throat cut, I'm coming to that if you give me a chance. There was a little errand boy poking about in the shop, and when we come out, though not to do with ourselves what Tomlin requested, he come running after us. So if you want it short and sweet, it cost me sixpence, but it seems that the other day, Wednesday morning which was, one of these coves that buys the Kentucky bacca asks Tomlin if this said boy could carry a message for him. Which he gives a penny for. And here's where the plot curdles.'

The aggravating monster paused for an effect. 'The boy was to go to the St. Martins's Tavern about twelve and ask for a Mr. Wilkes; and on Mr. Wilkes being pointed out to him he was to next ask, "What time does the clock strike?" Which upon Mr. Wilkes would reply, "Precisely on the hour, if it keep true", and the boy was then to tell him that the meeting had been changed from the regular place to The Hog In The Pound, Bully Wheeler's place.' He leered at me triumphantly. 'Which is what you reckon the cove on our doorstep tried to get out last night. So what d'you make of that?'

'Not a lot. It's plainly a password and countersign of some sort, but it don't tell us much until we know what it applies to. Though if there was a meeting at The Hog In The Pound it's villainy of some sort. Even so it's very likely no more than a bit of jiggery-pokery on some sporting event. You know what Bully Wheeler is.' This Wheeler being a most uncommon rascal, a mail coach driver at one time until he got turned off the road for his hell-and-be-damned driving; a sportsman of sorts, from

27

illicit cock-fighting to nobbled horse-racing and dubious pugilism, and up to every trick known to the Fancy. 'But unless I'm much mistaken, this affair goes deeper than Wheeler.'

Maggsy grunted. 'Wheeler'd go as deep as damnation if it suited him. Anyway, that's where Jaggs's gone. No sooner had the boy let that lot out than he says, "We got it, Maggsy—this is what we're looking for, and I'm off to The Hog. I know some of 'em there, and I'll soon discover what this clock's all about. You go back to The Bear to wait for the guv'nor, like he said, and tell him I'm hot on the scent and running with my nose down." '

'Be damned,' I said. I was considerably annoyed. 'Running with his britches down more likely, the blue-arsed, pink-snouted, half-spavined baboon. I'll have the hair off his head. God knows what mischief the goose-wit might do. At the least he'll tell 'em all at The Hog that I'm in the field. Couldn't you have stopped him?'

'Nobody couldn't have stopped him. I told him he'd get himself gutted if he wasn't careful, but he's starting to fancy himself at this detection. Seems he's catching it from you. And whoever it was planted that cove on our doorstep must know you'll be after him, so what does it matter? We discovered something for you anyway.'

I was bound to grant that. I never fail to give praise where praise is due. 'Something, maybe, though not a lot. But did you get this tobacco customer's name?'

Maggsy shook his head, somewhat uneasily. 'That's where it come unfortunate. We scarce had that bit about the clock before old Tomlin appeared roaring from the shop, bawling for the boy to come back or he'd cast him off the street out of his job. And never another word from him.'

I made several more thoughtful observations but then continued, 'I can see I shall have to have a few words with Mr. Tomlin myself, whether he's deliberately with-holding information or merely being contrary. So here are your own further instructions. You are to go to fifty-four Portman Square this afternoon, to see what you can glean about this Julia Bracegirdle, for I've a fine fat chicken to pick with that mysterious lady as well. And I hope to God . . . '

But what I hoped was never to be uttered, as precisely on that our ears were saluted by the richest Irish brogue you ever heard, which I shall not attempt to set down here for fear it might be incomprehensible. 'Glory be,' it cried, 'here's well met, Colonel Sturrock, sir.'

Maggsy muttered, 'I told you so,' for the man had approached close by us, and then I recognized the foxy-looking fellow at last, after near enough five years. It was the change from a dirty, stinking, ragged uniform to town clothes that had put me off. 'Be damned,' I said, not all that welcoming, 'Sergeant Clancy of the First Foot Brigade.'

'The same,' he announced, working himself down on the bench beside us without invitation. 'Begod, it's a handsome generosity in you to rimimber the name of a poor old soldier after so long, and a treat for eyes to see yourself so fine and proud. The last sight I had of you was on the fearful morn of Waterloo, when you was led off by a pipsqueak of a captain to be hanged for a Bonapartist spy. "And there goes a fine rare man, and God rest his soul," I says to my boys.' *

'And the first I saw of you,' I retorted, not to be outdone, 'was on the eve of the battle. You and your rascally platoon were busy purloining a keg of rum from a commissary wagon.'

'Ah, well, now,' said he, 'If you'll recollect, the wa-

---

*Suicide Most Foul

gon'd got itself tipped over someways. If we hadn't saved that rum for betters uses them, villains of the Coldstreams might've had it. And it was a fine soft night.'

'It was pissing with rain,' Maggsy observed feelingly.

As indeed it was; it had been a fine chapter of mystery which had led me, Jagger, and Maggsy to the tender mercies of this rascal's wife and her houseful of young ladies in Brussels—in short, a whore shop—and then on to the doubtful company of the fellow himself on the sodden battlefield.

He was the last person I had ever expected to see again, especially in The Brown Bear, and looking pretty prosperous after his own fashion. And I could have been well rid of him at this present, though I greeted him kindly enough. 'You came through the battle unscathed then?'

'All the way to Parus after the Frenchies,' he answered modestly. 'A trifle or so, to be sure. A cannon-ball or two and the mischancy musket shot and sabre slashes now and again, but nothing to speak of. I was close ahint Old Hookey's stirrup all the day, and still there at twinty minutes past seven of that bloody avening, when he took off his hat and waved it forrard and says, "Now's your chance, Sargint Clancy; on your way to Parus, my man." ' The lying rascal let out a sigh that damned near ruffled old Solomon the Receiver's beard, clear across the tap. 'Grand and glorious days, Colonel Sturrock, sir. We shall never see their like again.'

'I hope to God we don't.' I said. 'And plain Mr. Sturrock will do. I make no claim to military eminence. But how are you finding yourself in London now?'

He looked at me sideways. 'The blessings and bounties of peace. You know the way of it, sir. You're a rare hero when there's fighting to be done, but you can rot in the gutter whin it's all over.'

There was truth in that, and I was not without

sympathy, but far too fly to show to this fellow. I more
than suspected the Old Soldier's Touch, and I observed,
'You look well enough on it nonetheless.'

'Praise be to God and Mrs. Sargint Clancy,' he replied,
but I noted that he seemed somewhat uneasy, and not
only in his new clothes. 'There's a fine resourceful
creature. She brought her girls from Brussels and set
herself up in the most iligint little establishment in Parus
for the Occupation. But times was growing oncertain
with the end of it, and she says, "Mr. Sargint Clancy,
when all's said, there's no place like London." So here she
is now with a similar iligince in Panton Street, off the
Haymarket, and nothing but young ladies of a proper
rispictability. And all her savings in it, God prosper the
good woman.' But he broke off there to cry, 'Well,
begod, here's me forgetting my manners. Will you and
the young gintleman not take a little drop of something
with me to salute the occasion?'

Now here is a particular warning. Namely, never let
an Irishman or an old soldier purchase the first drink, for
if you do, you may be sure you will pay twice for it in the
end, and if it happens to be an old soldier, a sergeant, and
an Irishman all together be trebly careful. 'It's my tavern,' I said. 'I'll do the honours. Will you take a pint of
ale with us?'

I fancy the sergeant had his mind on something better,
since I was taking claret, but he was profuse in his
expressions of gratitude. And when that flood of elo-
quence had subsided, we came down to true business,
for he gave me his sideways look again and observed, 'I
wouldn't be listening to a gintleman's conversation save
by chance, but I couldn't help but hear some mention of
a certain unsalubrious public house in Oxford Street.'

I returned him look for look. 'You might well have
done. But what of it?'

'Well now . . . ' He waited while the serving wench

brought his pot over and flounced her tits at Master Maggsy. 'I have it in my mind that I might have heard a whisper, or maybe not just so much as a whisper, that there might be some oncommon queer mischief brewing in that quarter.'

'If it's anything like the liquor Bully Wheeler sells there it'll be damnation queer,' I said. 'But what mischief in particular?'

He peered at me over the rim of his pot. 'As to that, I wouldn't be sure. It's no more than a smell of it, if you take my meaning. To be plain and straightforward with ye, Mr. Sturrock, ever since that fearful night of Waterloo my mimory's been a little trifle mischancy. It seems to come and go with me. But does the name Thistlewood mane anything?'

It was as much as I could do to stop myself from pricking up my own ears. For Thistlewood was a known associate of the rabble-rouser Orator Hunt and both had been up to their eyes in the St. Peter's Field troubles last year. If he was in any way concerned with our present affair we might indeed have mischief on our hands. Nevertheless I said, 'And if *my* memory serves me correct, Sergeant Clancy, the day you're straightforward, the weathercock on top of St. Botolph's Church steeple will lay a brass egg. So to be brief with you, Sergeant Clancy, what d'you want?'

He contrived to look innocent reproach. 'Why would I be wanting anything at all now? Or no more than the pleasure of renewing old acquaintance. But I'll tell you the truth then,' he added with the engaging frankness of a costermonger about to sell you a rotten cabbage. 'It was Mrs. Sargint Clancy that proposed it. "Mr. Sargint," says she, "it's common knowledge that our old friend Mr. Sturrock's a fine big man in London these days, and I'd dearly like to pass the time of day with him again. Why don't you set out to look for the gintleman now, and tell

32

him that whinever the clock might suit him, there's a dish of tea and welcome for him here at Panton Street".'

There was no mistaking the message, and Maggsy very near gave away our interest. He turned his lascivious eyes from the serving wench to stare at Clancy with his mouth as wide open as the parish oven. But I said, 'And seemingly you knew where to find me easy enough.'

'And wouldn't that be common knowledge as well? I'll tell you the way of it, Mr. Sturrock. Me and the boys of the old platoon've kept togither. Whin we come back from the Occupation of Parus I says, "Now, my lads, I'll not see any of you starving in the gutter. There's this and that to be found here in London the same as Parus. You'll keep under my command and standing orders, and I'll see you don't want for much." ' He gave an Irishman's rich chuckle. 'Did I iver tell you what the Duke of Wellington, no less, said about the boys in Brussels? "Sargint Clancy," says old Hookey, "I don't know what your men'll do to the French, but by God they frighten me." '

'It was a famous remark,' I observed. 'From the number of times I've heard it, he must have made it on a score of occasions.'

'Maybe so. But you'll perceive how it is, Mr. Sturrock. An army marches on its intilligence, and the boys catch a whisper of this and that here and there.'

'Including some mischief brewing at The Hog In The Pound?' I enquired.

'It might be so.' He finished his ale thoughtfully and got up from the bench to leave us. 'Which brings to mind a touch of news consarning another small matter in Brussels. But I've a notion that Mrs. Sargint Clancy'd best like to give you that herself as she discovered it, and I'll not keep you any longer from your proper business.' Then, however, he turned back as if on a further sudden thought. 'Did I hear now that your man was away to The Hog?'

'You could have done,' I said. 'If you were listening hard enough.'

He nodded mysteriously. 'It was but something I caught. So I'll give you good day, sir. And bear in mind that Mrs. Sargint much hopes for the honour of you at Panton Street whin it suits you.'

'Well, God's sake,' Muggsy muttered, watching him edge out through the door. 'What d'you make of all that?'

'Why,' I said, 'if that amiable rogue were acting the stage Irishman on the boards at Drury Lane the critics would say he was overdoing his part. Nevertheless he's given us food for thought as he meant to do. So we'll take ourselves to Hackett's Eating House to digest it with our dinner.'

= 3 =

A PRETTY DECENT cut of sirloin, with apple pie and
Stilton to follow, though the mulled claret was by no
means all it might have been. You'd have thought that
with the war over these five years past the French might
be doing better with their wines. I suspected that the
rascals were sending us their worst out of revenge. Yet
after the damnable fog outside, the eating house was
warm and snug with its roaring fire, tall settles, and Mr.
Hackett himself enquiring after our comfort. So when
we had fully satisfied ourselves, we sat back to take a
breath, lit our pipes, and turned to a deeper consideration of our mystery.

'First,' I observed, 'it's plain that Clancy's heard of
something, and if it's concerned with that damned rabble-rouser Thistlewood there's mischief in it. It's just as
plain that he's fishing to sell the information. Though we
don't know yet what price he puts on it.'

Maggsy sniffed. 'By the way he spoke of Mrs. Clancy
and her new whore shop in near the same breath, that's
plain enough as well.'

'You mean protection of some kind? Be damned to
that. That's something a man in my position may not
descend to. Moreoever it's something that his Lordship
Jackass at Bow Street would fall over himself to get his
teeth into if he ever heard of it.'

'You ain't got no position now,' Maggsy pointed out

sourly. 'You can be like Caesar's wife if you fancy. All things to all men.'

'You're somewhat mixed in your classical allusions,' I told him. 'Let us continue. Second, it's by no means certain that our man on the doorstep and the other who sent Tomlin's boy with his message are one and the same. Tomlin claimed two customers for the Kentucky tobacco.'

'Well I'll lay odds on it,' the argumentative wretch said. 'Stands to reason. He was up to something with somebody and fell out with 'em, concluded to split on whatever it is because it's too rummy, so come to you but they catched him first. You can't have nothing more straightforward than that.'

'You put the matter in your usual elegant nutshell, but we'll assume it is so for the present. So where does that bring us?'

'God knows. But if somebody goes around gutting people on other people's doorsteps it means they're in a damnation hurry about something. And if it wasn't for Jaggs we'd do best to let it well alone. If he comes back with his head still on, you don't have to go roaring about now you're retired. But knowing you, I doubt you'll see sense and keep away from it, so the quickest way to find out is to ask Clancy what it's worth.'

'Be damned to that again,' I replied. 'Nobody but a fool would try to strike a bargain with Clancy or his woman, and we don't need either of 'em. We've got five items of our own to proceed on. The fatality itself; Cato and that bit of Latin about Carthage; Tomlin; the clock password; and Julia Bracegirdle, if there is such a woman. For I've a feeling in my bones that that mischievous letter to milord Jackass has some part in the affair. And, thick-wit as Jagger may be, even he might have something to tell us when he returns.'

'If he does return,' Maggsy said.

'Then if he don't that will tell us something, too.' I was growing impatient. 'So let's be about our business. You will take yourself to Portman Square to find anything anybody might know about the said Bracegirdle. While I shall go for a few words, kind or otherwise, with Mr. Tomlin the tobacconist.'

But it was a sleeveless errand. To put it brief, Tomlin proved confounded obstreperous. You would expect your tobacconist to be a jovial sort, full of thoughts of comfort and warm firesides—but not this fellow. And stage-post innkeepers are nearly all pretty much the same: off-handed, grasping, and indifferent when the tired traveller looks for a hearty welcome. With Tomlin, however, it was an ancient grudge, coming back from a time when I had purchased a pound of tobacco from him—my regular supply having failed me owing to a shipwreck—and then had occasion to enquire whether he was not mistakenly selling dried cattle dung.

It was expressed in the politest possible terms, but he seemed to take it unkindly, and there was no more kindness about him now. 'I don't bandy information about my customers to nobody,' he announced when I put my simple question. 'Much less to you,' he added for good measure.

'Come now, Mr. Tomlin, there's no need to harbour an old grudge,' I told him. 'Moreover, it won't pay you to. This is a matter of murder.'

'All the more reason for me to keep well out of it,' he said.

I hardened my own tone. 'I want that man's name. And it's a Bow Street matter.'

'Is it then?' The rude fellow gave me a malevolent grin. 'So let Bow Street find out.'

'Be damned, sir,' I said. 'What d'you mean by that?'

'Plain enough, ain't it?' he asked. 'News travels fast,

Mr. Sturrock, and I've heard you spoke of before today. One of the other Bow Street men was in here not an hour since. A gentleman who does me the favour of regular custom and speaks well of my goods. And out of favour to you I'll tell you his precise words. He said, "Wonders and miracles abound, Mr. Tomlin. Our bullfrog's got his leave at last. Sturrock's opened his big mouth too wide once too often and got his discharge from the force. And maybe that'll teach him to walk on his two flat feet like the rest of us, instead of acting the lordship with his chaise and coachman." '

It was uttered with evident intention to offend, and I was deeply mortified that I could have such a spiteful enemy among my own men, but there was little profit in exchanging pleasantries with a mere discourteous tradesman. I had thought of dropping the name Thistlewood to observe what effect it had, yet there was now even less in that, and I tried a fresh tack. I said, 'Well enough, Mr. Tomlin, if that's your mood. We shall see whether you're of the same mind when the clock strikes.'

He looked at me as if I had taken leave of my senses. 'Damned if I know what you're talking about,' he observed. 'Nor do I want to. So you be off about your business and leave me to mine. Don't go pestering my boy Ebenezer either, for his own sake. He's away on an errand now, but I've already warned him that if he gets chattering about any of my customers to you or anybody else he'll find himself back in the gutter again, where he comes from.'

'Well enough,' I repeated. 'But I'll advise you that you're sailing confounded close to the wind in dangerous waters. If you have any information you might disclose but won't, you might live to regret it. Or you might not.'

On that parting shot I took my leave with what dignity I could muster. I had lost a skirmish, but not the war; and Tomlin, I concluded, was merely an innocent though ill-tempered fool. There would be time to teach him better manners later. For the present I was pretty certain that he was withholding his customers' names simply out of spite and that my word about the clock had meant nothing to him, for he did not have the wit to dissemble. There was still the boy to find and question, whatever this blockhead shopkeeper might threaten, and that was a job best left to Master Maggsy.

And then I was strangely at a loss as I stepped out from the lighted shop into the darkness of the fog in Tottenham Court Road. The afternoon was now wearing on to half past four and commonly at this hour, if I had no other business on hand, I would return to Bow Street for reports and consultation on the day's affairs with old Abel Makepenny. But the thought came like a sudden blow that there was no place for me there now. True enough, nobody would dare to turn me away if I chose to present myself, but Abel knew by arrangement where to find me should he have anything to impart, and I was damned if I would go anywhere near that office again until I had his Lordship Jackass in person imploring me to return.

I stood irresolute for a minute. Me of all people, Jeremy Sturrock, considering like a useless idler what to do with his time, near oblivious to the half-seen figures of passersby groping their steps in the stinking yellow murk, barely noting the muffled clatter and dim lamps of what little traffic there was abroad. 'The devil take it,' I told myself, refusing an impudent torch boy's offer to light me on my way. 'This won't do. Yet it's too early to go back to Soho Square with nothing achieved. I'll try a shot at random in the St. Martin's Tavern,' I said; and on that sudden decision I turned off to my left to find St. Martin's Passage, which leads through from Charing Cross Road to the lane of that same name.

It was no more than a hundred yards or so, but well

before I found the corner—and it need looking for in that damned fog—I became aware that I was being followed. To turn this way from Tomlin's shop door I had to pass his window, and I had noticed a thin, cadaverous but muffled-up figure there, seemingly peering in at the array of snuff jars and tobacco canisters. I gave him no particular attention then, but as I paused to take my bearings by the light of another shop, I perceived that the fellow was still close by, pausing with me and then drawing back furtively into the darkness. 'So ho,' I said to myself, 'are you following me, my man? If you are, you're a fool and a novice at the game. And two can play it. We'll try it a step or two more and see how it goes.'

So I turned into the passage, which is a narrow unsavoury alley, as gloomy as the corridors of Hell though nothing like as warm. Here within a few yards it was blind man's buff, with no more than a ghostly yellow effulgence at the Tottenham Court end, and I paused once more in a convenient doorway to take another look back. I was now quite invisible, but I could see the man plain enough, or rather his strangely tall shape, against the misty glow there. He seemed somewhat uncertain, poor fellow, pausing again to peer into the darkness before entering the passage, as if he did not much fancy the job on hand; I reflected pleasantly that he would fancy it even less in a minute. Nevertheless I was puzzled, for rascals who mean mischief commonly hunt at least in couples, especially with me as the quarry; nor was it likely that he would have accomplices waiting somewhere here to set on me, since there was no way he could have known which way I might turn on leaving Tomlin's shop.

But all should be clear before long, I promised myself, still waiting for him. Once let me get my gentle forearm about his neck and he would wish to God he had never tried this adventure. He would explain himself fast enough, for, as Master Maggsy often observes, I am a damned dirty fighter when occasion demands. And so it might have turned out, with much or all explained, had it not been for the filthy habits of some of the vulgar alley dwellers of London.

Another minute and I would have had him in a sailor's cuddle. He was just abreast of me, all unconscious of his doom, pretty well feeling his way, and cursing poetically under his breath. It struck me again that he did not much care for the job but I was already reaching out to take him, when somewhere above us a window banged open and a shower of unspeakable filth descended. What it was I know not, but it stank like the Fleet Ditch. Being still in the shelter of the doorway, I escaped it, thank God—thus proving that the righteous may go unharmed—but it caught our blundering villain full and square, and I never saw a man so surprised and put out. 'Be damned to you,' he bellowed, to be answered rudely by a woman's voice from above; a rare, fine doxy by the sound of her. Staggering as he was, he was as blind as an owl in daylight, I might have had the rascal easier still then but held off for the stink and fear of soiling myself as well.

He offered up a short prayer in good, round, army language, and the woman screamed back, 'And likewise to you, so watch yourself, my coney, for there's plenty more where that comes from.' She added several more choice epithets, to which our man replied in kind, while I cried above the clamour, 'Hold hard there, madam. And what d'you think *you're* about?' I then demanded of the unhappy rascal. 'What the devil do you mean by following me?'

It was a needless question, and it received a curious answer. Still cursing and spitting, trying vainly to shake and brush off the filth, he stopped for breath and announced simply, 'Bugger you, Sturrock—and double bugger the Sergeant as well.' And on that he turned and fled back towards Tottenham Court.

Neither was there any profit in lingering myself, for the woman was still leaning out of the window above and cackling with vulgar laughter. Discretion was the better part of remonstrance, and I called, 'Pray hold your fire for a minute, madam,' while edging away close to the wall. I was torn between vexation and a certain amusement. On one hand some rascal of Sergeant Clancy's old platoon had received a salutation he little expected, though on the other I had not got as much information as I had hoped for. Yet I had discovered that the curious Sergeant was having me observed for some mysterious purpose of his own. As Master Maggsy might have remarked, the plot was curdling even more.

There was no other incident, but I was thankful when I emerged from that noisome alley to see the lights of the Tavern beckoning me across St. Martin's Lane. This is a place much frequented by the middling sort of actor—as the better kind patronise the literary coffeehouses, where they may exhibit themselves to admiring country visitors—and I am well known to many of them as a singularly well-informed play-goer. And so occurred the next vexation of that vexing day, for one pompous old ass caught sight of me as I entered; a tedious, fat ham-bone who could never be content with a simple greeting but must need always make a performance of it. 'What ho,' cried he in a voice like an echoing tombstone, 'who approaches anon? 'Tis none other than our critic of the Thespian Art, Brother Sturrock, late of Bow Street. By the pricking of my thumbs, something wicked this way comes.'

So the news had reached here also, and I could have felled the fat barrel of piss and port for announcing it so loud. But I returned his salutation just as amiable with the retort courteous. 'Begod, Mr. Legrande,' I said, 'are you still here then? I'd heard that Sadlers Wells had offered you the chance of your life as the hinder parts of a horse.'

It was the best I could think of on the instant, but it served its purpose to disengage me from the group about this fellow. I had more important business on hand than exchanging pleasantries with out-of-work actors, especially as in this unfortunate position they all suffer from the Thirst Prodigious. I was looking more for one of the tapmen and another Irishman; a halfway rascal known as Limping Mick. In exchange for certain information some time since, I had extricated this simple soul from a little naughtiness that might have got him transported, and he was not ungrateful; moreover, he still had a fair notion of which side his bread was buttered on.

I found myself a settle in a secluded corner and passed the word for Mick by the serving wench. She looked at me somewhat sideways herself, for that damned actor had a delivery that was reputed to once have fetched the plaster off the wall at the back of the gallery in Covent Garden, and by now everybody in the place knew who I was. But the mischief was done with no way to undo it, as Mick also showed plain enough when he appeared at last. Half saucy and the better half uneasy, he greeted me, 'It's a fine benefit to see you, Mr. Sturrock, but I'm uncommon busy today, and the guv'nor's got an eye to me.'

'So have I, Mick,' I told him. 'And you ain't so busy that you might not yet be idle for a long time to come.'

He shook his head, and had the impudence to grin with it. 'Not now, Mr. Sturrock. You can't do that now, not by what I'm hearing.'

'Don't be misled by what you hear, Mick.' I smiled at him kindly. 'I've my own reasons for letting that tale get about, and I can still let slip a word or two in the right quarters. So let's be quick and have simple questions and short answers. And here's the first. Do you know of a certain Mr. Wilkes, and is he here today?'

His face shut up like a banker's front door. 'I niver heard of the gentleman.'

'Did you not?' I held my smile, which has frightened the liver out of many a harder villain than Limping Mick before now. 'So we'll let that pass then. So we'll try a little riddle-me-dee. What do you hear about a clock, Mick? Which clock—and when does it strike?'

I fancied that he knew of something there, but not much, or not what it meant, for his face had a come-and-go touch of intelligence and then a look of honest puzzlement—or as near to honest as he could get. He shook his head again. 'So help me, Mr. Sturrock, I dunno what that is at all.'

'You ain't just all that bright in your wits today, are you Mick?' I asked. 'You'll have to do better if you want to save yourself, my lad. But I'm a patient man, and I'll give you one more chance. So tell me now, what do you know of another gentleman who might call himself Cato?'

And, by God, that did frighten him. The fellow was transfixed. 'Cato?' he repeated. 'That ain't . . . ' he started but stopped short, first staring at me and then peering round fearfully over his shoulder. 'God's sake,' he muttered, 'the guv'nor's looking for me.'

'Let him look,' I answered. 'I'm another customer. Cato,' I prompted him. 'That ain't . . . that ain't what, Mick?'

He shook his head once more, desperately this time. The way he was going he would shake it clean off in a minute. 'See now, Mr. Sturrock,' he whispered, 'I'm obliged to you. You know that. If you mean to get me transported, you may please yourself. I'd as soon a

Botany Trip as see my throat cut. Nor I wouldn't give a lot for yours neither if you're meddlesome. Leave it be, sir.'

'So you could tell me something,' I said. 'Very well, Mick. It's your choice between a chance on your throat or a surety for your neck. I'll give you till tomorrow. You know where to find me, and I know where to find you. If I recollect correctly, it's above Watkins' fodder store in the Long Acre.'

He cast another look about over his shoulder, then leaned over the table to me, speaking in a low and hurried voice. 'Listen now, Mr. Sturrock. I can't tell you nothing, as I don't know nothing but for whispers I've heard—and them not meant for me neither. And if I could, the devil I would then. If they're after what I think it is, by God I'll wish 'em luck of it. It's time and more than time for a change. Beyont that I won't say and can't. Except maybe a word to the wise. It might be better away to the country than here in London for a while to come.'

Upon that he snatched up the empty pots from the table and bustled off, calling out cheerfully, 'Coming, gentlemen, coming begod. Be damned, have I got a dozen hands then? I can't serve all of ye at once . . . ' And left me thinking profoundly.

Profound and disquieting thought, which lasted me all the way back to Soho Square; and more than time enough to spare for it, as there was never a hackney to be had for love or money and I was forced to walk. It was not all that distance, but made twice as far by the fearful confusion: blundering pedestrians and impatient horses, lamps, torches, and wagons, etc., the end of your own nose well-nigh invisible, and your life at dreadful risk when you dared to cross the streets. Dr. Johnson has observed that the man who is tired of London is tired of life, but I cursed the place and all its shadowy inhabitants to hell and back that damnable February afternoon.

At least I was pretty sure that I was no longer followed. Sergeant Clancy was hardly likely to have set more than one of his men after me, and just as well. I had matters of greater import to consider now, and I was in a quandarious situation, for I had come to a fair notion of what devilish mischief was brewing: Clancy's mention of the firebrand Radical, Thistlewood; the inner meaning of the words *Delenda est Carthago;* the password and countersign of the clock, indicating a conspiratorial gang or assembly; and Limping Mick's warning to leave London. The precise significance of Cato still escaped me, though clearly it was not simply a pseudonym for one or another of the villains concerned, but all the rest could only be taken together to one end—an end far more wicked than a mere sporting plot hatched at The Hog In The Pound. Therefore my duty as a rightful citizen was all too plain. I should report the matter instantly to the proper authority.

Aye, and there's the rub. For the proper and immediate authority was Bow Street.

Was ever a man so torn between duty and his decent self-esteem? Moreover, even if I could mortify myself so far as to bring it before milord Jackass, I had little doubt of how he would receive it and me. At best he would dismiss it as no more than a fantastical suspicion; at worst he would fancy that I was trying to crawl back into favour on my knees. True enough, if I demeaned myself so far, he might set one of our lesser men to investigate and much good that would do, considering some of 'em. Just as true that if the conspiracy were allowed to come to its end, I could claim that I had already warned the Magistrate but what good would there be in that either? And what might the end be? I hardly dared contemplate it, yet in the present state of unrest all about us there was clearly one very dreadful danger.

It was a serious decision, but at last I said, 'Tomorrow.' If my instincts and observations were correct—and they are seldom otherwise—the plot was not yet fully ripe, and I might still have a little time. 'Be damned,' I told myself, 'it's my mystery, and I've the best right to it. Tomorrow I'll set about Limping Mick once more, and I'll extract what he knows if I have to strangle him with his own guts to get it. So also can Maggsy find that boy of Tomlin's again. Moreover, by now Jagger should have returned, and it's not impossible that even he might have discovered something. Likewise tomorrow old Abel Makepenny is to sup with me at Hackett's. So I can then lay the whole matter before him, and we can decide between ourselves what's best to do.' Thus so often does mere man propose, while Providence disposes.

By this time I was thankfully near to home, turning out of Charing Cross Road into Sutton Street, which comes out into Soho Square on the other side from my chambers. And here I came upon the first sign of the curious dispositions of that said Providence. For even in the pervading gloom I could see a strange glow through the fog across the square, shifting shadows, and other signs of commotion close by my own front door; voices raised, and Master Maggsy's unlovely accents above them all. 'Heaven help us,' I demanded aloud, 'what have they done now? Have they set the place afire?'

'Go easy with him,' Maggsy screeched; and as I hastened closer, the shadows grew more solid into a knot of those useless idlers who in London are always attracted to calamity, like flies to carrion. Lanterns and torches bobbing among 'em, a dejected horse that looked as if it was near dropping to its knees with despair, and a rude box-vehicle which appeared most horribly like the mortuary van. 'Lift him tinderly now,' I heard in Sergeant

Clancy's Irish brogue, while Maggsy screeched again, 'Stand away, God blast you,' and the horse neighed mournfully in sympathy. 'Is it a dead'n?' one ghoulish voice enquired, and another answered, 'Ain't far off by the looks of him.' And being carried across the pavement to our door a horrid, limp, and dripping bundle.

'What in damnation is this?' I roared, loud enough to silence them all, and in the sudden hush which followed, Maggsy snarled back, 'Plain enough ain't it? Jaggs's come home—and not in the best of health, neither.'

—4—

'WHAT IS ALL THIS?' I demanded again when at last they had the unfortunate fellow upstairs and laid on the sofa in our sitting room. It was a scene of some confusion in the lamplight. Jagger himself seemingly as dead as a log and dribbling stinking water everywhere—that good sofa would never be the same again; Sergeant Clancy more than ever like an Irish fox; several shifty-looking rascals whom I took to be some of his men; our household woman, Mrs. Odcock, caterwauling at the door; Mrs. Spilsbury's man, Grommet, peering round her; and Maggsy cursing fervently. 'Be quiet, the lot of you,' I cried, and then demanded again of Clancy, 'What happened to Jagger and how do you come here?'

'Why, sir,' Clancy replied, 'as to the first part, it seems the poor soul went to someplace he'd have been the better off of not going and as to the second, to make a brief of a long tale, me and some of my boys found him in the Paddington Canal. But if you'll pardon an old soldier's expayrience you'll do best to look to the poor dear man first and leave explinations till later. He just ain't at his finest and fit to fight.'

And that was all too evident. Jagger had never been much of a picture, even in robust health, although he had seemed to please several young women sufficiently at one time or another, but now he looked like something drowned, buried, and somewhat carelessly dug up again.

Of a pallid, greenish hue, his eyes half shut and mouth hanging open, liberally besmeared with muck and slime—I never saw anything less like a sporting coachman. 'Pore old Jaggs,' Maggsy sniveled, 'he's got a lump on the back of his head near as big as a duck egg, and he's copped it like I knowed he would.'

But as I bent closer to examine the good brave fellow he gave an unearthly little belch, fetched up a mouthful more of water, and I cried, 'There's life in him yet. The rascal's got a head like a solid oak.' I began to issue orders. 'You, Mrs. Odcock, stop that damned noise and go to get hot blankets on his bed. And take yourself off out of this, Grommet, or I'll throw you out. Clancy, have your men strip the wet clothes off him. And you get the brandy, Maggsy, and then run to fetch Doctor Pentecost out of Greek Street.'

'Go gintle with him, boys, for he's a bit tinder,' said Clancy, while Mrs. Odcock and Grommet scuttled off and Maggsy darted to the wine cupboard. 'But let the young gintleman hold a minute, Mr. Sturrock,' the Sergeant added. "Ye'll not want a horse leech to the poor fella, sir. Any one of them hack-bones'll just be after bleeding him and have him petered before you've time to say a prayer for his soul. I've took the liberty of sending a runner for Mrs. Sargint Clancy.'

Once again on that dreadful day I was dumbfounded. 'You've done what? By God, my man, you take too much upon yourself!'

'Wisht now, sir,' the impudent scoundrel answered, 'say no more of it. It's a little bit of a thing to do for a gintleman like yourself, and the good woman's had a fine expayrience. Has she not followed the army for better of seventeen years, since she was a slip of a girl? There's nothing a common quack-salver might do that she'll not do better. Ain't that the truth of it, boys?'

'Oncommon true,' one of them replied, heaving off

Jagger's sodden britches. 'We've seen her as good as raise the dead.'

'That be damned,' I said, seizing the brandy Maggsy was bringing and giving myself a strong dose. I could see the trap this rascal was leading me up to, yet there was a certain sense in what he said. The woman might easy do better than Dr. Pentecost; while if I was to discover what information Master Clancy had, the surest way would be to give him a bit of sailing room first and then tack about to catch him on a leeshore. I moderated my tone somewhat. 'Nonetheless I don't fancy Pentecost all that much myself, and I well remember how Mrs. Clancy tended the wounded after Waterloo—as good as any of the officers' fine ladies. When may we expect her?'

'Any minute now.' He gave me his foxy grin, thinking he had me well on course. 'I sent her word that the matter was desprit.'

'So we'll let it rest at that,' I agreed handsomely. 'And I'm obliged to you. But before she comes, tell me—how did you contrive to find Jagger so fortunate?'

'A matter of chance and a nod here and there,' the rogue replied unblushingly. 'It so happened that I took a bit of a walk the way of The Hog, being arranged to meet some of my boys. Which further so happened that my Corporal Pikestaff caught a sight of some fella that he knows there, and had a brief discussion with this same in the yard at the back. Upon that, one small word led to another, as you might say, to the end that we next upon commandeered a tradesman's van and went the way of the new Paddington Dock. Corporal Pikestaff's a fine fast driver when we're on manoeuvres. And would you believe it, but there we found your good man. Not much above waterlogged, as seemingly he'd had the last wit to catch a hold of a tangle of ropes to keep his head up. Twas little short of a holy miracle.'

'Not so much a miracle as your resourcefulness,' I said

warmly. 'And you'll not find me ungrateful. But I wonder what the devil he was doing to get himself into this kind of trouble? Did you not say that you'd had a hint of some sort of mischief at The Hog?'

Clancy shook his head and at the same time cast a warning glance at his men, who were still busy stripping Jagger. 'Bedamned, sir, no more than a hint, or maybe not so much. That's a queer shop, so it is. And so many various divilments there that who's to tell which from what?'

'I fancy he had some kind of notion about a clock,' I mused. 'Might that be timing for a horse or a coach race? Jagger's a restless, sporting rascal with the horses, and it's a well-known interest with Bully Wheeler as well. Did you ever hear of a horse called Cato?'

The shot went close enough, but being a true old soldier Clancy showed little sign of it. 'It's a queer old name to anything,' he said.

'Indeed it is, these days,' I agreed. 'But it's no great matter.' They had Jagger stripped by now, a singularly unpleasing spectacle, and I continued, 'Very likely this good fellow can explain it when he recovers. If he does. If Mrs. Clancy can resuscitate him, you may ask pretty near anything of me within reason. A good coachman's hard to come by these days. But if she don't I shall be exceedingly displeased. And for God's sake, get the blankets from Mrs. Odcock to cover him,' I added to Maggsy.

'She'll save him sure enough,' Clancy said, though I fancied there was an uneasy note in his voice. 'He ain't got much more than half of the Paddington Canal in him, and we emptied most of that out. And begod, here she is now.' For as he spoke there was an imperious clanging on our doorbell, with Mrs. Odcock quacking on the stairs and a minute later Mrs. Sergeant Clancy making her entry.

And an entry it was, with another, younger, woman behind her; as good as Drury Lane. You'd have thought she was the Colonel's Lady at least. As I remembered her in Brussels she had seemed very near as big as the side of a house, weatherbeaten and brawny, and workaday clothes, a fine figure of a washerwoman. But now the very pink and complexion to modishness, and even a touch of Paris about it, though nothing extravagant. An elegant bonnet and overmantle, a silk and fur muff and fine gloves, and a ladyship manner as genteel as her attire. 'Good evening to you, Mr. Sturrock, and pray permit me to observe that I find it a peculiar pleasure to renew your acquaintance,' she announced in the most precise of tones, while Clancy gave me a strangely hangdog grin.

'Your servant, ma'am,' said I, not to be outdone in the genteels, and now taking in the younger woman she had brought with her. Master Maggsy was already goggling at the vision, with his eyes like billiard balls, and you could hardly blame him for it. Just as modish in her style—and if Mrs. Clancy was the Colonel's Lady there was little doubt that this innocent creature could be none other than his daughter. Too damned innocent by half, I reckoned. About eighteen to twenty, as pretty as a picture by Mr. Gainsborough, a maidenly bloom on her cheek and one or two well-disposed curls escaping from her hat, a look as if butter wouldn't melt in her mouth; and not to be trusted an inch.

But Milady Clancy was taking the boards. 'And this is our patient?' she enquired. 'No doubt a fine constitution if he were in better health. I like to see a good strapping figure.' She bent over to examine Jagger more closely, while the younger woman regarded him just as unblushing though all Miss Demurity otherwise. But I am bound to confess that both of 'em seemed to know what they were about when they set to do their business. 'The breathing's uneasy and rasping, but it might be worse, and you'll perceive a considerable contusion here, Ermina,' Mrs. Clancy announced. 'It seems the young man's been keeping undesirable company; yet there's no bone broken or depressed so far as I can discover. He's very likely got a skull like a cannonball. Young men of this build frequently have.'

Master Maggsy chose to answer that with a less than half-suppressed snigger, but she quelled the wretch with a single look and addressed herself to me. 'Very well, Mr. Sturrock, I think we may save him if we're quick enough. Pray instruct your woman to bring blankets and put hot bricks or a warming pan to his bed. Then she may lead the way while you have your men carry him there, Sergeant Clancy. After that, return with them to Panton Street, if you please. I don't care to leave our young ladies unattended in these restless times. You may take the carriage to make haste, but send it back for me.'

I began to understand Clancy's touch of the hangdogs. I was damned near breathless myself, and the other rascals was pretty well standing to attention. But as if she were born to it, Mrs. Sergeant Clancy continued, 'I shall remain here until he seems better composed, Mr. Sturrock. And then when we're sure of that, Miss Ermina will sit with him. With your approval,' she put in as a kind afterthought. 'He'll need constant attention, and she'll not inconvenience you.'

'Quite so, ma'am,' I answered, now starting to wonder if I was bereft of both my wits and my tongue while Sergeant Clancy muttered, 'Stand to there,' and Maggsy said hurriedly, 'I'll go to hasten Mrs. Odcock along with them blankets.'

'Dear God,' I observed simply but with profound feeling, when all the performance was done and Maggsy and me were left with the sitting room to ourselves again.

'Likewise Godamighty,' echoed Maggsy. 'Or does she reckon she is? And a town kerridge, if you please. And did you never see anything like that Miss Ermina?' He gave an evil leer. 'Pickle me sideways, I dunno what Jaggs'll do when he comes about and sees that sitting beside him. Or I've got a notion. But what d'you reckon they're at?'

'Get the Madeira out,' I ordered, as near at my last breath as Jagger himself. 'I'm in need of a restorative. And it's as plain as the nose on your face what they're at. They mean to discover what Jagger saw or heard, or conversely what he did not see or hear, at The Hog In The Pound.'

'So are they with us or against us?' That I could not answer, or not yet, and Maggsy nodded mysteriously. 'So I'll tell you something else you don't know. You recollect that you come roaring up as they was getting Jaggs out of that van? Well, I'd only got there a minute before, myself, coming back from Portman Square.'

'Ah yes,' I said. 'Portman Square and Julia Bracegirdle. What did you glean of her? I hope to God something's turned out right today.'

'What I'm telling you now is that this van was a bit ahead of me turning the corner here to come round to our door. Which it's uncommon quiet on account of the fog, nor I couldn't see much, but I could hear it plain enough. So likewise d'you recollect what Jaggs said after you very near blowed his head off last night, I mean after his expected observations? He said he hadn't seen nothing, but he'd heard something with a bit of a rattle going out of our square by way of Sutton Street, and the horse a bit dab footed, like it might have been a shoe coming loose.' He paused for his inevitable effect, pouring out the Madeira and looking at me mysteriously again. 'Which is precise and exact what I heard when that van turned the corner.'

I stared back at him. 'You're proposing it was the same van that might have carried away our unknown corpse last night? And that Clancy or his men might then have been driving it?'

'I ain't saying nothing. It's you that says things. A lot of these vans've got a rattle to 'em, and there might be any number of horses with a shoe loose. But I ain't done yet. So when I come up to it there's already three or four torches and lanterns around, and I says, "God's whiskers, what's going on here," and Sergeant Clancy says . . ." '

'Spare the dramatics,' I checked him testily. 'I noted 'em all myself. Come to the nub of it.'

'Well enough. So I ain't so obfuscated that I don't take a good look at that van. And there, lettered on the side of it, was, "Jacob Spragg, Soap and Tallow Dealer, Watkins' Yard, Long Acre".'

'Watkins' Yard,' I repeated, thinking instantly of Limping Mick's address. 'So ho. And so ho again. I wouldn't be certain, but you might have done very well.' I considered it for a minute and then announced, 'And tomorrow you shall take it further. You shall go after Tomlin's boy again. And there must be more enquiries at Watkins' Yard.'

'Doing me a rare favour, ain't you?' he asked. 'I don't like this lot. There's somebody on the go damnation fast here, and they don't stop for compliments. I don't fancy getting done as well.'

'Anybody who could do for you could tie a knot in an eel,' I observed. 'Now then, let's come to Portman Square and Julia Bracegirdle. Did you discover anything about her, or who she might be?'

'Depends on what you make of it. Fifty-four's a select lodging house, but there's nobody of that name knowed there. I got to talking to one of the maidservants at the area door, and it seems they don't have many customers at this time of the year. No more'n four now. An old lady who's permanent, and halfway to Bedlam, though nice natured with it. A cove who talks like he might be a parson, and another gentleman, which both do a lot of confabulating and discussing together. And another lady who says she's come from Paris, which said maidservant reckons ain't just such a lady as she lets on, but the one who might be a parson's plainly took a fancy to her. Name of Miss Letitia Merritt.'

'That's very near as improbable as Julia Bracegirdle.' I said. 'That's an assumed name for certain, and near as certain that there we have our woman. But we must let Miss Letitia Merritt wait for a while. Confound it, I could do with half a dozen men.'

'We could do with being well out of it. I keep telling you, there's somebody going too quick for my liking.'

'That be damned,' I said. 'I mean to get to the bottom of this, and we've made a fair start. We've got Clancy, Tomlin's boy, and Limping Mick. They must all be made to talk, especially Clancy. You'll note that Mrs. Clancy was uncommon quick to get him out of here tonight.'

Maggsy gave another of his horrid sniffs. 'We might have made a fair start but there's still somebody else a long way ahead. What I'm concerned about is who's going to get gutted next.'

And I am here bound to confess that in the light of later events the argumentative wretch's forebodings were fearfully prophetic.

To come to those events as soon as may be, I shall pass over the rest of that tedious evening as brief as I can. After an hour or so the already mentioned Corporal Pikestaff appeared; seemingly Mrs. Clancy's coachman, a dour and silent man who looked as if he had been carved somewhat carelessly out of an ancient gatepost, and just about as talkative. He sat by our fire and consumed an inordinate amount of my Madeira, but otherwise never uttered more than two or three words at a time.

At eight o'clock the lady herself descended to inform us kindly that Jagger was now in a more natural sleep, but must not on any account be disturbed, awakened, or questioned, or she would not be answerable for the consequences. I was a trifle constrained to answer her as courtesy required, especially seeing Maggsy's evil grin, but I begged her to take a glass of Madeira, which she was kindly pleased to accept, and then she informed us that she would return in the morning. 'There'll be little change tonight,' said she, 'and he's in excellent hands with Miss Ermina.'

'I don't doubt it,' I agreed, somewhat heavily. I thought of enquiring what was the news that Clancy said she had for me; something concerning Brussels. But that was five years back. I was more concerned with present questions, and after further politeness, waiting until she was drawing on her gloves, I asked suddenly, 'Pray tell me, ma'am, is Sergeant Clancy acquainted with a person known as Limping Mick, at the St. Martin's Tavern?'

She seemed to consider it. 'That I cannot say, sir. The Sergeant has a great many acquaintances. But why do you ask?'

'The fellow might throw some light on Jagger's misadventures,' I said. 'Though it's no great matter. I mean to question him myself tomorrow.'

I was pretty certain that the name conveyed nothing to her, but I fancied I caught a look of something on Corporal Pikestaff's wooden countenance. It was come and gone in an instant as they took their leave, and then Maggsy asked, 'Foxing again, are you—what did you loose that one at 'em for?'

'Another shot at random,' I replied, 'We shall see what it produces.'

So to bed and a sound sleep—for I hold that lack of it never yet solved any mysteries—and up again betimes with several fresh plans in hand. But first I went to enquire after Jagger; though to no effect, as I was met at the door by Miss Ermina with a finger to her lips, and still as demure as a buttercup. By the manner of the creature you'd have thought our sporting simpleton was about to give birth, and me the perplexed father. Yes, she whispered, he was much improved, but, no, he had not yet uttered a word, and still must not be disturbed. 'Well enough, m'dear,' I said. 'And I've no doubt that when he wakes to see you sitting beside him he'll fancy he's in Heaven.'

Next to a good solid breakfast, with the fog outside as damnable thick as ever, and then to dispatch Master Maggsy about his errands while I went about my own— in short, to the St. Giles Mortuary once more. I had not had any message from Jonah Gotobed there, and it was time to remind the rascal, though I was coming to consider that we might have to do without the identity of the unfortunate fellow on our doorstep if it took too long to discover. He had served a purpose with his broken words and tobacco pouch, and at need he could be left to rest now as we followed the hotter scent.

Nevertheless Jonah Gotobed must still be repri-manded. I cannot put up with the lower sort taking upon themselves what they will or will not do, and I spoke my mind when he came stumping out of his office to greet me. 'Jonah,' I said, 'don't seek to butter me with your fanciful welcomes. You're an impudent rogue. And don't take a notion that you can play please yourself because I've seen fit to change my situation from Bow Street to a higher authority. Did I not tell you that I wanted certain information and wanted it quick? So where is it, my man?'

'God's truth, Mr. Sturrock,' he cried in a fluster, 'no offense intended. I'd meant to let you have a word, but we've been so pushed with this fog. Either it chokes 'em or they come by haccidents. Three fresh clients last night, and the van gone not ten minutes since to fetch another in. I ain't forgot your request—it's a pleasure and a privilege. But I dunno that what I have got for you comes to much.'

'I'll be the judge of that,' I told him.

He looked at me shifty from his one eye. 'It's but a word or two that I picked up, and I wished it was more. It'd be an honour and a privilege to do for you, Mr. Sturrock. Nor I don't swear it's your hunfortunate accident neither. But I did happen to hear that a certain delivery was took to the back entrance of St. Bart's Hospital late of Thursday night. Which same delivery the anatomy rooms porter refused, seeing there was suspicious appearances about it, but advised the certain persons consarned to carry it further to Dr. Astley Cooper. And to be sure to tell him who recommended it.'

'Astley Cooper?' I repeated. 'The anatomist?'

'The same, sir. And a regular customer to certain trades.' He nodded meaningly. 'I see you knows of him.'

'Who don't?' For he was the foremost anatomist of the last twenty years, First Surgeon at Guy's Hospital, Lecturer in Anatomy at St. Thomas's, and not a man lightly to cross swords with. The tales told about him were legion. It was well known that he would sink his knives into anything from a mouse to an elephant, and indeed as long ago as 1801 he had actually cut up one of those monstrous animals in a public show outside his house at St. Mary Axe, in the City. The demonstration was a nine-day wonder at the time. It was said also that he liked to pass two or three hours in the dissecting rooms every morning before breakfast and that he regarded it as criminal madness to allow any young apprentice surgeon to approach a living body before he had learned his business on the dead. As Gotobed had observed, a regular customer to certain unsavoury trades; and for all that, he never failed to speak his mind about the Resurrection Men—as about most other things—he paid the rascals well for his subjects. 'Astley Cooper,' I said again. 'Be damned to that.'

Gotobed nodded once more, uneasily. 'And so say I. Mr. Cooper's demands're well knowed. He wants a fresh'n every day, and ain't partic'lar how he gets it. If I might venture, sir, seeing your man was took to him of Thursday night, if it was your man, there won't be a lot left by now.'

'By God there won't,' I said. 'And confound you, Gotobed, I hold you responsible. If you'd let me know this sooner I might have learned something. But now you've baulked me, damn your eyes, and I'll not forget it.'

The creeping rogue very near wrung his hands off in agitation. 'God help us, Mr. Sturrock, what could I do? I never knowed it myself till last night, and I told you, sir, I been that pressed I don't know how to turn. Three of 'em yesterday. A young boy first, and then an old trollop come asking after him, claimed she was his grandmother and demanded his clothes. After that another fellow, both accidents, and both from Long Acre, which struck me curious. And next a youngish woman . . . '

Displeased as I was, still considering Mr. Astley Cooper and our lost man, there was a word or two there which caught my ear. 'Wait,' I commanded Gotobed, with a sudden horrid suspicion. 'Did you say a young boy, and Long Acre?'

'That's right, sir. Sorrowful.' He shook his head this time. 'Found in the gutter. Seems got himself under a

Covent Garden wagon in the fog. You'll know the ways of . . .'

'Hold your clapping tongue,' I said, 'and let me see him.'

'To be sure,' he cried, all eagerness again. 'It's a pleasure to oblige when I can. Step this way, sir.'

There was no surety of it when I surveyed the sad mortality under its rough canvas shroud. A very commonplace small boy, and there are thousands of the wretches infesting the streets of London, but I had little doubt that Master Maggsy was now engaged on a sleeveless errand. 'You'll know how it is,' Gotobed was babbling again as I looked down on the poor naked urchin. 'They get running after the wagons to thieve what they can, and the carter flicks his whip at 'em, and then they slip, and that's . . . '

I cut him short once more. 'Hold your tongue, or talk to some effect. You say an old woman came asking after him. Did you have his name? And was he some kind of shop boy?'

'Firkin. I got it in my book. And right again, sir. The old bags spoke of some shop in Charing Cross and her only stay and support. Which most consarned her.' He heaved a doleful sigh. 'It's a sad wonder, the way the poor live.'

'What's more to the point is the way they die,' I observed, finishing my brief examination. 'Very well. Now let me see the other from Long Acre.'

This time there was no doubt at all. A single glance sufficed, and few short words. 'If you don't have this one in your damned book I can tell you. Known as Limping Mick. Was a potman at the St. Martin's Tavern. And most likely reported to you as having broke his neck falling from a hayloft above Watkins' Yard.'

'Begod,' Gotobed announced, 'there's right enough as

well. You're a rare marvel and wonder, Mr. Sturrock. Never no need to tell you anything. You know it all to start with.'

I gave him a sharp look, but he seemed guileless. 'It's my business to know. And I mean to know more yet. So answer me careful now. What time was this man brought in last night?'

'A bit after ten. I was about sitting to my supper and an hour with my Bible. I always like an Holy text or two to suit my clients here. They don't get much else.'

A bit after ten. And had it been just before nine when I told Mrs. Clancy to pass the word that I meant to talk with Limping Mick today. So had she passed it to this end? Had Sergeant Clancy or some of his men done for Limping Mick, and therefore, by a simple connection, for the boy as well? If they had, they must have worked damnation fast, at least in the case of Mick. But Master Maggsy had already observed that somebody here was as fast as the Devil himself, and always a step or two ahead. 'So we come back to the boy,' I said. 'What time was he brought?'

'Near enough five of the afternoon.'

'And no doubt sitting to your Prayer Book then.' But at five o'clock Clancy and several more of his men were busy bringing Jagger back from the Paddington Canal. Yet an hour or so before that he had had one other man following me close by Long Acre; and where there was one, might there not have been another, engaged about a different business? There was no answer to that presently, but several aspects were all too plain. That if Clancy were concerned, he was merely an underling, for he was not of the stature to encompass such a considerable conspiracy as I now saw clear; that the chief villains, whosoever thay might be, were prepared to strike without mercy, and on a breath of suspicion, even at the lowest and simplest; and that if they were working so fast and ruthless, their plans must be close on coming to a head.

I was seriously perturbed and put further questions to Gotobed but gained little more. Both the boy and Limping Mick had been dead when found, and no witnesses. There never are. The boy, reported to the Parish Constable by a passerby unknown; the other discovered by the street Watchman on his rounds. And, considering what all Watchmen and Parish Constables are by nature, there was little hope of learning much from those quarters. 'So there we have it,' I pronounced at last. 'When are the inquests?'

'Not hinformed yet, sir. Today being Saturday, most like day after tomorrow under Dr. Busby. He'll rattle 'em off like shelling peas.' The fellow looked at me as eager as a spaniel. 'Why, sir? Would you wish to be present?'

'Be damned if I would,' I answered. 'I've got better things to do. Death by misadventure best suit all parties concerned. And, Jonah,' I added, 'if you value your life by a ha'penny, don't breathe a word to anybody about my interest. Not even to your Holy Bible.' I gave him my most benevolent smile. 'Otherwise you might well find yourself lying on one of your own slabs there.'

=5=

THE DEVIL OF it was what to set about next. Even could I find a hackney to take me as far as the City in this confounded fog, there would be small hope of finding Dr. Astley Cooper, as by this time he would be at one or another of the hospitals or otherwise engaged in his curious works, and I might waste half the day looking for him. Moreover I was pretty certain now that that scent was cold and best abandoned unless it freshened again. So with two more of my game also driven to earth, I had only Clancy and Jagger left. As for Jagger, God help us; but Mrs. Clancy might be caught at my chambers, and on that thought I turned my steps back to Soho Square.

From which arose a further curious incident. It was not far to go—though through several dark streets—before I reached the busyness of Tottenham Court corner, but I had scarcely left the mortuary before I perceived that once more I was followed. The unsavoury stews of St. Giles close by, little traffic here; narrow alleys and old and dilapidated buildings huddled close together; shadowy figures appearing out of the murk and vanishing back into it, and, clear enough in the quiet, the tread of furtive but purposeful footsteps behind. I know that sound from long experience, for not even the wild Indian knows the murmurs of his forest better than I know those of London. 'So ho,' said I, 'Sergeant Clancy still at his tricks—and this time we'll have an end of 'em.'

But some quick stratagem was called for, and before I could decide on that there was a fresh sound behind, enough to set your teeth on edge; somebody whistling "Lilliburlero" shrilly and out of tune. When I glanced back, there was a fitful glow of light, growing brighter as it approached, and then a most horrible little street Arab about twelve years old. As filthy as a mudlark, an impudent gap-toothed face, an ancient beaver hat too big for him crammed over his ears, disgusting green frock coat hanging down to his ankles, bearing a crossing sweeper's broom over one shoulder and a torch in the other hand. 'Light your way, guv'nor?' the apparition enquired.

'Be off with you,' I told him. 'I know it well enough.'

'Lay odds you don't,' he replied. 'Lay odds you dunno there's a couple o' footpads follering you, neither.'

'I know that as well,' I said. 'Take yourself off.'

He gave me a wicked grin. 'Least ways they look like footpads. I seen you come out from the mortewry, and they was waiting agin the wall. I could dash 'em in the chaps with me torch for ye. That'd steady 'em!'

I advised him what might happen to his own chaps in a minute, but short of breaking his neck you might as well try to brush away a leech as one of these wretches when he attaches himself. The creature fell in, a pace or two behind me, and started his damnable whistling again but then broke off suddenly to ask, 'Be you Sturrock?'

'I am,' I said. 'D'you fancy a night or two in Newgate?'

'Catch me fust,' he announced, whistling a few more staves. 'Bleedin' fog,' he observed next. 'Coves like you gets footpadded in fogs like this. Rare for trade though. I made fourpence yesterday.'

I was still listening for the rascals behind, considering how best to trap them, and the child was beginning to vex me. 'You'll make a boot in your arse if you don't get out from under my feet.'

'Catch me fust,' he answered again. 'Anyways, if you'm Sturrock, I got a messidge for yer. Name o' Cato. Summat consarning a shop boy of old Tomlin's.'

'What?' I demanded. 'What's that?'

I reached out to catch the scruff of his neck, but the wretch was even quicker and slipped away, haloed in the flare of his torch like an imp out of Hell. 'Wuth a sixpence, is it?' he asked.

'It might be,' I said, edging closer, torn between this little monster and the fellows behind. 'It might be worth more. You give me the message and we'll see.'

'Catch me fust,' he chanted once more, and darted off, near invisible in an instant, again like the aforesaid imp.

'A shilling,' I said after him. 'Hold there a minute, you little bastard,' but there was no answer save his horrible piercing whistle and the fitful glow of his torch.

'Catch me fust,' floated back out of the gloom, while at the same time I heard the footsteps behind again. It was a quick choice which to take up. But Cato was more important than Clancy, and I was incensed. I meant to have that little wretch's guts as well as whatever he might tell me, and I started after him like a blind traveller following a Jack o' Lantern. Near enough at a trot, though it is dangerous to go too fast in St. Giles. Down one street and around a corner to the next, I ran through one pestilent alley and out to another, bumping into shadows and answering curse with curse, discouraging one importunate ruffian with a cut of my cane, sweeping away a bedraggled old witch who screeched unseemly objurgations at me, trampling through a mass of something that stank like rotten cabbage or worse, falling into the grip of another woman even more drabbish than the first, sending her flying and squealing in her own skirts, and always with that impertinent whistling and the flicker of the light just ahead.

It was a devil's dance in a maze, and how long it

continued I cannot say, but all of a sudden the whistling ceased, the light vanished as if a door had closed on it, and I shall confess that I was fairly cozened. Me, Jeremy Sturrock, with all my wits about me, to fall victim to a mere street urchin. I had no notion of where I might be, save that it was well inside the rookery—of which nobody living knows all the labyrinths, for the denizens there make holes and burrows like rats—and seemingly in a little enclosed court, as murky as the inside of a sow's belly and a good bit more stenchsome. What little I could see was dirt, disorder, and ruin, and I shall not record what I said in praise of that wicked child as I stood there peering about. There was no movement, and all was quiet for a minute, but then the whistling started once more and the glow of light appeared again, now as if behind a grimy window.

I could smell danger and feel it, but by this time I was so enraged that all caution went to the winds. I said, 'I'll have you now, by God,' and plunged through a half-seen doorway into some kind of dark hovel, and into the hands of the villains waiting there for me.

The torch was gone, and they fell on me in an instant. Four or five of 'em at least, though I did not stop to count, for they meant quick murder with no niceties. More by sense than sight I struck away a vicious cudgel, then lashed back just as wicked with my weighted Malacca—without which no gentleman should go abroad in London these days. That fetched a crack of bone and smothered shriek, but one rascal got a clutch at my throat. I brought my knee up to him, I fancy to the considerable detriment of his privates, judging by his sudden cry of anguish. Another tried to drag me down from behind, muttering, 'Finish it, blast ye, Spadger— where's yer knife?' then ending that in a sour belch as I drove my elbow back in his guts. 'Not so fast,' said I, with another lash of my Malacca at a half-seen face.

Yet hit back as I might, and I can fight as dirty as the best when occasion demands, the odds were against me. I can take on two at any time, three if I must, but four or five in the dark is too many. Even so they did not have it all their own way. I cracked one rogue's skull for certain, severely discommoded another, and bloodied several more before the end came. It was a mere chance, a frightful blow at my head, but it knocked me dizzy. I went down making several observations, though expecting the end and still determined to sell my life damnation dear.

Then, however, I seemed to note a strangely increased uproar. So far the affair had been pretty quiet, but now it broke into a fiendish mix. Trampling feet all about me, and none too careful with it, further blows, imprecations and curses, crashing and splintering, and all the indications of a very fine general mêlée. My last thought was that Master Maggsy must have somehow joined in the fray, for only he could cause such hellish confusion so quickly.

After that I knew no more until I strangely discovered myself being half carried, half dragged through the streets again, and at rude and inconvenient pace. A figure on either side supporting me, far from gentle, and plainly impatient. My last thought had been that Master Maggsy had joined in the battle, and now my first was that the villains were carrying me off to finish the business in some quieter place. On that all my fight returned to me. Though still bemused, and swaying somewhat, I shook one of 'em off boldly and turned on the other with my fists up, demanding, 'Want more yet, do you, you damned rascals—come on then.'

'Begod, Corp'ral, he's come to,' said that one, to which the other replied, 'About time,' and added, 'Stand easy now.'

'Stand easy? Corporal?' I repeated, blinking the blear

out of my eyes, and scarce able to believe them. For it was the wooden countenance of Corporal Pikestaff haloed in the fog, and now set in a look of some disapproval, a most displeasing sight. 'What in damnation are you doing here?'

'Orders,' he answered briefly. 'Keep a hold of him, Private Potter, or he'll fall again.'

'Be damned to you,' I retorted. 'What happened to those rascals who set about me? Where are they?'

Private Potter gave a singularly foolish titter. 'God knows. As to what happened to 'em, you near enough killed one, broke another's arm for'n, and pretty well crippled another for life.'

'Confound this,' I said. 'If you've let 'em escape, you'll hear more of it. I wanted one at least.'

'You'm a rare wicked fighter,' observed Private Potter in simple admiration, but the Corporal barked, 'Silence there, Potter,' and then added to me, 'Reckon yourself fortunate. There was two more left, and but for us they'd've knifed you.'

'But for you?' I said. 'Don't you think I could've settled with 'em myself?'

'No,' he answered. 'You was laid out like a drunken dragoon.'

'Damn your impudence,' I said. 'And your eyes. And how the devil did you come there, and why? What were you about?' He did not condescend to reply to that, and I continued, 'There was a boy. A most horrible little street urchin with a torch. Did you see the boy there?'

'That's right,' announced Private Potter. 'We seen him right enough. He follered you from the mort'ry. Seems he was waiting for you.'

'Silence in the ranks, Potter,' Pikestaff barked again. 'For your information, there wasn't no boy in that position as we advanced on it. He'd made himself scarce.'

'As well he might. But by God I'll have the little devil

found. And when I do . . . ' I paused for breath, bereft of speech by the thought of what I would do with him, but then demanded, 'So where's Clancy? I want a word or two with him now.'

'We has no information on Sergeant Clancy's present whereabouts,' said Corporal Pikestaff. 'We has our orders and we carries 'em out. And that's all. You fell into a hambush already prepared, and fortunate that we come up as rearguard. Which is the long and short of it.' He paused on that himself as we turned a corner, which I now perceived took us into Drury Lane, and no more than a few steps from the hospitable portals of The Brown Bear. Then he enquired, 'Permission for escort to dismiss?'

'Permission granted,' I replied in the same manner. 'But report to Sergeant Clancy that I require a word or two with him before the day's out. I've no doubt he'll know precisely where to find me.'

As further misfortune would have it, Master Maggsy was already present when I entered. He was exchanging impertinent pleasantries with Polly, the serving wench, but they both broke off short at the sight of me; she uttering a little squeal and Maggsy gazing with a look of something as near concern as he could ever get. 'God's whiskers, at it again?' he started, but stopped short. 'How many of 'em?' he asked at last, and then, 'Looks like an army. I hope you gave 'em as good as you got.'

'Better,' I answered. 'Five at least. Bring me some brandy,' I added to the wench. 'And don't stint it.'

Maggsy nodded with a sort of gloomy satisfaction. 'Never learn, do you? Lost your hat as well. And made a rare mess of your coat.' I noted then that there was a long knife cut down the left front. 'Didn't have to get a lot closer, did they? I keep telling you, this lot's wicked. D'you know what happened to Tomlin's boy?'

'I know,' I said. 'Let it be for a minute.'

But in the end I told him the whole tale. A sorry story it was, for no man likes to confess that he's been made a fool of, much less me, and he listened in unwonted silence until I finished. 'It was the word "Cato" that caught me. I'd chance anything to know the meaning of that. There's no doubt that the boy was set on to tease me into the trap, and instructed precisely how to do it. And Clancy's careless rascals did not trouble to save one of the villains for me. Had we but got only one of 'em we might have had our fingers on the whole mystery by now.'

He shook his head. 'Dunno about that, neither. By what you reckon there's somebody a lot higher up than St. Giles coves and shop boys at the back of it. That sort don't do the jobs themselves. They pay others, and don't tell 'em why.'

'So much is clear, even to me.' I took the brandy thankfully. 'All the same I'll have that boy found.'

'Not by me you won't. I don't fancy being another sorrowful accident.' He put on his look of mulish obstinacy. 'Besides he's very likely got his head knocked in by now as well. Seems to me this lot picks on somebody to do a bit of something for them and then says, "Thank you kindly, and off you go." See now, you've done your best and very near got gutted for it. I reckon we should go back to the chambers and stop there till Jaggs is up and around again. This ain't no weather to go rollicking about in, anyway. Then Jaggs could drive us off out of this. We could go to Bath if you fancied it. That's where there's always plenty of nobility and gentry, and if you're still looking for mischief, which you can't help doing, you could find it there respectable.'

He paused for breath, and I said, 'That be damned. I'll see the end of this affair if it's the last thing I ever do.'

'Very likely will be,' he interjected.

'And the prime thing now,' I continued, 'is to find out what Clancy's tricks mean.'

'That's plain enough, ain't it? Following you around to see that you don't come to no harm, which is uncommon obliging, except there's no reason why he should be. So if you ask me, he's got wind of something, but don't know what it is no more than you, and reckons on you to find out so he can get his pickings from it if there are any. And I'll lay Mrs. Clancy put him up to the notion.'

'I fancy you're right in that at least. But the rest ain't good enough.' I finished the brandy and felt much recovered for it. 'There's fair reason to consider that he might be an underling in the business himself. And I do know what it is, as I've already told you. However, we'll go back to Soho Square in a minute to see what we can get out of that fine lady, or the other saucy little trollop. But first, what did you discover about the tradesman's van in Watkins' Yard?'

'Something and nothing,' he said. 'That's the van right enough, which wasn't present in the yard then, but Jacob Spragg the Soap and Tallow Dealer's dead these two years past, died natural of the gin, and a cove named Pocock's got it now and lets it out on hire. Which was gleaned from a stable-hand, said Pocock likewise not being present. Asked where he might be found if any-body wanted this van, the stable-hand says anywhere between Hell and Houndsditch. Asked further if the horse's got a shoe working loose, he says if you can call it a horse it's going to cast the fore offside any minute.'

'As you say, not a lot,' I observed. 'But continue.'

'Well then, said stable hand demands to know what am I after anyway, so I let on nothing special, but I'm looking for a respectable van to take my poor old grand-mother for her funeral, to which he gives a leery kind of grin and says it wouldn't be the first time it'd been used for that, and not so respectable neither. Which I done the innocent and asks him what does he mean, and he says to ask Pocock if that's my business, as he don't want nothing to do with it.'

'So that means the Resurrection Men use Pocock's van. But it don't take us far.' I considered that for a minute, and then reflected on Limping Mick meeting his death at or near this place, and the time of it. 'Did he say anything about any other occurrences at Watkins' Yard lately?'

'Didn't have time. Somebody inside roared at him what the hell did he reckon he was doing, leaning on his fork and clapping his idle tongue, and he went back to mucking out quick, and I come away.' Maggsy gave me a suspicious look. 'Why? Has anything else happened there?'

'Nothing of any note.' I thought it best not to tell him too much about Limping Mick's unfortunate misadventure yet awhile. He would have to go back to Watkins' Yard again before long, and he was already in a sufficiently nervous and rebellious mood. I returned to the matter of Tomlin's boy, though to little purpose. Maggsy had discovered no more than I had learned for myself, except that seemingly the boy had last been seen alive about three of the afternoon in Covent Garden.

'Nor does that get us much further,' I observed at last. 'I might try Tomlin again myself if I have time, but I doubt we shall get much more out of him. For now we'll go back to Soho Square to see what we can extract from Mrs. Clancy or Miss Ermina.'

But not a lot of good out of that either. Our Mrs. Odcock was in a fine fluster, and Mrs. Clancy been and gone an hour before, but at least Jagger was now awake and talking, with Miss Ermina still sitting by him. 'And by God he shall talk,' I announced, 'when I've tidied myself and changed my clothes.'

So, with these necessities attended to first, I took myself to Jagger's attic chamber—and uncommon comfortable quarters for a coachman, better than he might have had in many a noble household—to find a scene of domestic bliss that very near took my breath away. Jagger reclining on his pillows like a lord, wearing such an idiotic grin as turned your stomach over; Maggsy perched on the bed and likewise grinning, but in his own wicked manner, and at lewd thoughts; and Miss Ermina sitting by it with a look on her face like a cat that's got at the cream. I could have had all three of 'em out of the window, but I said kindly, 'Well, Jagger my lad, I see you're looking more like yourself.'

'Oh, indeed, sir,' says Miss Demurity. 'A most wonderful recovery.'

'No doubt due to your tender ministrations,' I observed, which fetched an indecent snort from Master Maggsy. I fixed that wretch with a look that wiped the smirk off his chaps, and continued, 'I mean, Jagger, that you look a bigger bloody fool even than God ever made you. And He must get a bit bemused sometimes when He considers his handiwork.'

'La, sir,' cried the trollop, now like a cat defending her young, 'That's no way to address an invalid.'

'Invalid be damned,' I said. 'Moreoever, miss, I shall address my own coachman as I please. Though first I'll have a word or two with you. But not in the presence of this blue-arsed, spotted-rumped, simple-witted baboon. Downstairs, if you please.'

'Here,' Jagger bawled, 'You go easy,' while Miss Ermina stuck her saucy nose up at me to announce, 'I do not care for your manner, sir.'

'No more do a lot of rascals,' I told the hussy. 'And they like it less when they find themselves lodged in Newgate.'

'You lay off her,' Jagger roared again. 'She ain't no

rascal, nor she ain't going to Newgate neither.' But Maggsy muttered, 'Let it be, Jaggs, he ain't in the best of tempers,' and added, 'Best go with him, Miss Ermina. He's had one or two little vexations today, and I wouldn't answer for it if he gets any more.'

'Very well,' said she, 'if I'm so advised politely.' She cocked her snout at me again and gathered up her mantle and various other female appurtenances, announced, '*Au 'voir*,' Mr. Jagger, and I pray your full recovery will not be too much disturbed,' and then gave me a rare fine touch of the duchess. '*If* you please, sir,' and marched down the stairs before me like it is said the French aristocrats went to the guillotine.

'Very good, my dear,' I observed when I closed the door behind her in our sitting room. 'I've never seen a prettier performance. Mrs. Siddons herself couldn't have done it better, and she's a lady I much admire. But now we'll talk quiet and friendly, shall we?'

She gave an upward shift of the snout again. 'I'm quite at a loss to know what you require of me, sir.'

'That's what I'm about to explain, my dear,' I told her, as amiable as a kindly uncle with his favorite niece. 'You and me can talk like a lady and gentleman for a minute or two now, and you mustn't be fretted by a few rough epithets for Jagger's benefit. They're what the good fellow's used to, and what he expects. You might call them expressions of endearment, but we mustn't spoil him. It don't do to spoil a coachman, however high your regard. Between the two of us, he'll take advantage if he gets the chance. So I want him to fancy that I've sent you packing back to Mrs. Clancy.'

'But, sir,' she started, and I held up my hand to stop her.

'I know precisely what you're going to say. All the same, you should take a rest by now, and I'm certain you'll be more at ease with Mrs. Clancy than sitting here all day long in rough bachelor chambers. I hear on all sides that she keeps a most genteel establishment, and she's like a mother to you.'

'Indeed, sir, she does, and she is.' The pretty creature very near gave me a smile, not quite trusting yet but getting on the way. There are few ladies can resist me when I put on that tone. 'We all go to church on Sundays, and we occupy every afternoon with writing and improving literature. Mrs. Clancy says she sees no reason ladies should not be quite as well informed as gentlemen.'

'No more do I. And I've no doubt you're very well informed. Have you heard the latest conundrum that's going about? What would you say if I asked you when does the clock strike?'

She frowned like a child over that for a minute, but then shook her head. 'I fear I don't know, sir.' I had not expected her to tell me if she did, but very plainly it meant nothing to her. 'What is the answer, sir?' she asked.

'Hardly worth the telling,' I said. 'Something to the effect that it depends on whether it keeps good time. It's a mere foolish question fashionable among gentlemen lately. So you've never heard one ask it of another?'

She shook her head once more. 'Never, sir. I fear Mrs. Clancy would consider it more suitable for the nursery.'

'And so it is. I've no doubt your discussions are on more elevated matters. But tell me something else if you will. Mrs. Clancy is plainly a very busy lady, as you all must be. I'm at a loss to understand why she should devote so much time and care to my man, Jagger.'

'Why, sir, that's very simple. It seems she conceived an affection for him some years past in Brussels. And an admiration for yourself.'

This time I was damned certain that she was only telling me the half of it. There was a wary look in her eye, but I did not press her. I said, 'I'm uncommonly obliged to her for the kindness, and to you. You may be sure that I shall look for some way to return it. And considering that, I mustn't keep you here too long in idle chatter. But there is one small favour more.' It was another shot at random, but worth the chance. 'It's an impertinent question, and very likely you won't care to answer it, for no lady likes to discuss gentlemen when they're not present. Nevertheless, I've a particular friend who speaks most glowingly of an establishment he's recently discovered, but so jealous of it that he won't tell even me where it is.'

I gave a rueful little laugh. 'And I'm jealous of him, as well. I'll not mention names, but he smokes a most rare and aromatic tobacco. I'm wondering if it's Mrs. Clancy's house.'

'Gentlemen,' she observed, 'do not smoke tobacco in the company of ladies.'

'Well, no,' I agreed. 'Not in the common way. But I fancy Mrs. Clancy understands the weaknesses of the sex, and I daresay she's got a smoking room set aside for their comfort. Nor I wouldn't be surprised if you young ladies ventured in there now and again. However, it doesn't matter all that much, though I'd like to surprise my good old friend. I'd like to say to him, "So ho, my fine fellow, I've discovered your secret haven." '

She fell into the trap like a kitten, though a bit doubtful at first, and I got more than I had dared to hope for. 'It might be,' she murmured. 'Mrs. Clancy declares it's a most *clinging* aroma. Perhaps I should not tell you. But is it Mr. Lampeter?'

I shook my head, even looking somewhat crestfallen. 'No,' I said. 'That's not it. I don't know of a Mr. Lampeter. So my old friend, Cato, will still have the laugh of me.'

I watched her closely, but there was no slightest doubt that that did not mean much to her either. Had she known or even heard of it before she'd have shown some sign. But she only repeated, 'Cato? What a very strange name.'

'There,' I cried, affecting a sort of amused vexation, 'I've given it away after all. I fancy you're a young lady who could get very near anything out of me. But so it is strange. My old friend's father was much taken by the ancient Romans and named all three sons after them. There's one brother, Cicero, and another called Juvenal. But they're only forenames,' I added, 'and I mustn't keep you from your well-earned rest any longer. I shall send Maggsy down now, and he'll find a hackney and escort you back to Panton Street.'

'There's no need of that . . . ' she began, and considering Maggsy, nobody could blame her, but I had my own intentions. I replied, 'It's the least we can do, dear,' and removed myself before she could argue further.

Returned to Jagger's room, I gave Maggsy his instructions, and for once he did not complain much about them, but seemed even to regard squiring Miss Ermina as an agreeable diversion. He observed, 'What ho, Jaggs,' and I warned him, 'Not so much of that. Mind your manners and use your wits instead. What you're after is polite conversation. Mention a Mr. Lampeter and in particular, don't forget what I've told you about Bow Street.'

'I've got it plain enough,' he retorted. 'It's only been put about that you've had a disagreement and been retired. That's a gammon, and the truth of it is that you've been sent up to a most special and secret government service. And swear Miss Ermina to it that she won't tell nobody. If you ask me, that'll start more mischief than we've got already, but please yourself.' He gave Jagger a lewd wink. '*Au 'voir*, Jaggs, like the lady said. It's my turn now.'

'I'll have your bloody head off before I've done with you,' Jagger bellowed at him as he departed, but I said, 'That's enough from you, my lad. By the strength of your lungs your ain't near so invalidish as you make out. I don't know what that trollop did to cure you, but I can hazard a fair guess, and if you're good enough for her sort of romps you're good enough to be up and about. But first, what have you got to say for yourself?'

'Ain't a lot I can say, is there?' he growled. 'Save that you didn't need to have blowed off at me like that. Nor at Miss Ermina. She's a rare kind young lady, and I've took a fancy to her.'

'Then you're a bigger simpleton even than you look. You'd take a fancy to anything with a pair of tits, and God knows she's got 'em well for'ard of the mainmast— and she's got bigger and better fish than you to fry. She wasn't here for your good, nor mine. So now let's talk sense for a bit. I want everything that happened when you went to The Hog In The Pound. Everything you might have seen, and every word that was said.'

The poor good fellow fingered the back of his head tenderly. 'Begod I never got the chance to see or hear much. I went in there friendly and open and says, "What cheer, gentlemen all." ' Bully Wheeler was standing there in his red weskit, and I says, "Is there anybody here can tell me what time does the clock strike?" And God help us, after that I didn't know nothing more. Not till I thought somebody was trying to pump water out of me somewhere, and then till the next time when I woke up here with Miss Ermina sitting beside me.' His face assumed the look of belly-turning idiocy once more. 'Like a hangel out of Heaven.'

'Then Heaven's a damned curious place,' I snapped at

him. 'I said let's talk sense for a bit. Something must have happened betweent the minute you opened your big mouth and the instant you got that blow on the head.'

He furrowed his brow in painful thought. 'That's right, come to reflect on it. Two or three together—stopped their talk to look at me. Then two of 'em come over by me, and one asks, "Where did you get that from, my man?" and I says, "Why, Tomlin's boy." '

I gazed at him consideringly, but out of kindness forebore from telling him what had befallen that unhappy child. Master Maggsy would inform him soon enough. 'You're doing very well,' I said. 'And what else?'

He beamed at me with simple pleasure. 'I ain't such a muggins. Now I come to recollect, Bully Wheeler says, "Not in my house," a bit sharpish. And I'm pretty sure somebody else says something about Marylebone. I reckoned that was to do with cricket. But then the bloody place fell on me.'

'Jagger,' I told him, 'you're a rare wonder. The world'd be a sadder place without you. But cudgel your brains a bit more. The two that came over by you, now. What manner was they? The lower sort? The sporting fancy? Or could they pass as gentlemen?'

'Can't hardly tell these days can you? They says, "My man," which is the way gentry addresses you. Reckon they was, or near enough, to look at.'

'And who else was present? Was there anybody known to you?'

'One or two, maybe. Nobody of no account. Jem Loftus, who's a harness hand with Lady Cutsdean's stable. And a cove named Bragg, who claims he'd been a groom with Lord Harrowby, but fell out with the first coachman. All mouth and wind.'

'Lord Harrowby?' I repeated. 'We're coming up to High Society now. He's in the government. Lord President of the Council.'

Jagger grunted. 'Dunno nothing about him. But as for this cove, I reckon it's Bragg by name and brag by nature. He was very likely no more'n a muck slinger, if that.'

'Keep to your observations,' I told him. 'Who else did you note?'

'There was three or four Dandies, horseflesh and pugilistic and racing fancy. The sort that's forever about with Bully Wheeler. And a lady. Leastways a woman, as no lady'd be seen dead in The Hog. But done up to the fashion.' He furrowed his troubled brow again. 'I got a notion that I knowed the cut of her somehow, but I never had no more's a glimpse of her, and she turned away. But there was something about that back.'

'It's something about the front that means most to you,' I said. 'Can you recall any more?'

'Be damned,' he cried, 'it was all over and done with in five minutes. I ain't got eyes in my arse as well. Leave me be, guv'nor. You're setting off my head again.'

'You're fortunate you've still got one,' I told him. 'Not that you make much use of it. Very well, my lad, you may have your rest out today, for you still look pretty gruesome. But I want you on the road again tomorrow. I want the men, Loftus and Bragg, found and brought to me.'

—6—

So Jagger had unwittingly provided certain food for thought. Not a lot, but my sure instinct told me that there was something here to nibble at to see whether there was any flavour in it, and I mused for a time on the mention of Lord Harrowby. I knew little about the gentleman, beyond that he was high up in Government—I mean the true Government, far above the mere quarrelsome rabble of Members of Parliament—but I had no doubt that old Abel Makepenny could inform me better, for he was a walking compendium on such matters. Yet whatever he might tell me, I was still getting too little certain information and too many uncertain hints, and time was treading even closer at my heels.

But Providence, in the strange shape of Master Maggsy, is always waiting to stretch out His hand to the righteous; although it was better than an hour before the wretch chose to appear. He marched in with an unholy smirk on his face again, as pleased as Punch with himself, and a sore temptation to me at that minute. 'I done very well,' he announced. 'Got an hackney after a bit, the fog ain't so bad now, and had a most genteel conversation. My eye, that Miss Ermina's got her head screwed on the business way. She says Mrs. Clancy's going to marry her to a duke or something before she's done, she's training her special for it, and if our Jaggs got a bit of what I think he got, I reckon he ought to consider himself . . .'

'Be damned to what you reckon,' I interjected. 'Let me have your report.'

'That's what I'm coming to.' He seemed curiously impressed. 'God's whiskers, I dunno how you done. You're a proper marvel now and again. But you got it right enough. It looks like this Mr. Lampeter's your man on the doorstep.'

I looked back at him, to tell the truth, marvelling myself that a mere chance shot had found its mark. But I preserved a decent modesty. 'All my observations leaned that way. If they're now confirmed it's the best news we could wish for. Are you sure of it?'

'Can't never be sure of nothing, can you? But first go off, he's an American, or was. Which accounts for the partic'lar tobacco. Next, he's been going to Mrs. Clancy's every Thursday night for the last three months or more and most polite and considerate with it as he's took a fancy to one of the other young ladies and never fails to send her word if he can't come. But he never appeared last Thursday, nor they didn't have no message, this being somewhat surprising. Which is when we found him, if it was him, on the doorstep. Well, he wasn't in no condition to go, was he?'

'It looks like a true bill,' I said. 'Is there anything else?'

'Not a lot, but ain't that enough? Never contented, are you? Miss Ermina didn't know where he lived, nor much about him otherwise, as his special young lady at Panton Street is Miss Rosana. But all agree that he's a very proper gentleman. Which Mrs. Clancy considers the same, and has a fondness for him, except she don't approve of some of his opinions.'

We were getting warmer, I thought, coming closer to my own suspicions. 'And what are those?'

'I didn't ask. I had to be a bit circumspectious. I told you, Miss Ermina's nobody's simpleton. I says everybody can have his own opinions if he wants to, but it's always best to keep your mouth tight shut on 'em. We was getting on famously in the hackney by then, and she gives a little laugh, and says but that's precisely what Mr. Lampeter would not do, and she personally don't blame him when you consider the way a certain Fat Man at Brighton carries on, which she holds is not respectable. But Mrs. Clancy reproved him for it, and says politics is best kept to the clubs and coffeehouses.'

'A certain Fat Man at Brighton,' I mused. 'So he made a habit of talking against the King.' I reflected on that for a minute and then announced, 'I believe I can see a bit of daylight at last. But we've still far to go yet. Does Miss Ermina know what happened to him?'

Maggsy shook his head decisively. 'Never a notion. Nor I didn't tell her neither. It ain't the sort of thing you do tell a pretty young lady in an hackney.'

'But I'm damned sure Mrs. Clancy and the Sergeant know it well enough,' I said. 'They've known it from the start. And I fancy I can now perceive what they want with me. As I say, I can see a touch of daylight, and you've found it. You've done very well.'

'That's what I said, I reckon so myself. But likewise credit where credit's due,' he added handsomely. 'You spotted it first. And for the life of me I still can't fathom how you done it.'

'Experience and profound thought,' I told him. 'Nevertheless, there's still much to discover. But at least we can now see part of the way.'

The first step was to descend on Mrs. Clancy, and accordingly I presented myself at Panton Street at the respectable hour of four in the afternoon. The door was opened to me by a fellow who had all the markings of another old soldier, who received me very civil and at once said, 'Very good, sir, be pleased to step this way.' It appeared that Sergeant Clancy boasted all sorts in his old platoon, for this man might have been taken for the proper sort of manservant except for his build, which clearly indicated the other duties sometimes called for in these establishments.

It also seemed that I was expected, as he led me into a pretty little anteroom, which again was very different from your common whore shop. Most 'em are excessively opulent to vulgar, but this was done out quiet and restrained: elegant French Empire furniture, three or four very decent pictures, and not too much of anything. It would not have disgraced my friend Lady Dorothea Hookham-Dashwood herself, and I hold her to be the epitome of refined modern taste. Mrs. Clancy, I reflected, had learned much while in Paris.

Nor did she keep me waiting for much above a quarter of an hour, which is about long enough for politeness from a lady, and when she entered she affected a most pleased surprise. 'Why, Mr. Sturrock,' said she, 'this is an entirely unexpected pleasure. And how does Mr. Jagger continue?'

'Wonderfully well, ma'am,' I assured her. 'Thanks to you and Miss Ermina.'

'She is a dear soothing child.' The good lady shook her head at me. 'But I fear she feels that you dismissed her somewhat sharply.'

'By no means, ma'am.' I protested. 'I was at pains to make that plain.'

She smiled at me graciously. 'Pray speak no more of it. But will you take a dish of tea?'

'Thankee, but no, ma'am.' I was just as gracious. 'I'm pressed for other business. And I fancy you know what it is. In short, Mr. Lampeter.'

She looked at me steady but said nothing, and I continued, 'I shall speak very plain. You and Sergeant Clancy both are well aware of what happened to that gentleman. You both are just as well aware of what might happen to you if enquiry reveals that he was a constant visitor here. You know the way of the world as well as I do. It's clear that you keep a most discreet establishment, but in the eyes of the Law this is still a disorderly house. And in matters of murder such places are always prime targets for suspicion.'

I paused to let her take that in, though she could see the way I was driving. 'Hence Sergeant Clancy sought me out yesterday, hence you both seized the opportunity to put me under obligation as regards Jagger. A cat's-paw to take the chestnuts from the fire for you, lest you should find yourselves in need of my experience and protection. And if I'm any judge there's something more as well. So what is it?'

She did not answer that. Instead she asked, 'How did you learn that Mr. Lampeter was a constant visitor? I trust Ermina's not been chattering.'

'No ma'am,' I said. 'Miss Ermina's not a young lady to chatter. It's my profession to discover things. So I'll now propose an end of subterfuge between us. You need my assistance, and I shall be thankful for yours. I'll tell you openly what I know, and just as openly confess what I don't.'

'Very well,' said she, though still wary.

'First, I know that Mr. Lampeter was a man of strong Republican opinions. They're commonplace among Americans, as I appreciate from several such good friends of my own. Nor he didn't hesitate to air his views, and in so doing he fell in with certain persons who reckoned he would be a worthy recruit to their cause. I fancy the fact that he was an American made them all the more eager to have him.'

'He did not fall in with such persons in this house.'

'I'm well aware of that. The centre of this mischief is elsewhere, and Mr. Lampeter found his own way to it. But from all I hear of him he was a kindly and decent gentleman. He held his opinions firm, but was not prepared to see 'em taken as far as these villains mean to go. In brief, he learned of a conspiracy which he would not stomach, and concluded to come to me to give warning of it. How he knew of me might or might not appear later. But I'm certain that he meant to come unknown and go away again unknown. Is that much correct?'

'I'm not entirely sure. But I think it very likely.'

'We may say that it is. So I must now put a number of questions; and plain answers will serve both of us best. How much do you, and how much does Sergeant Clancy know of this conspiracy?'

'I know little or nothing. I can only tell you that some days ago the Sergeant said, 'There's a bad business afoot that you're better well out of, Mrs. Clancy. If it comes to a head it might ruin us. But if I can say I've put a finger in to stop it, we might have a considerable benefit.'

I nodded benevolently. 'Mysterious, but much as I expected. Now tell me if you please—was Sergeant Clancy in or near a place called Watkins' Yard, in Long Acre, between nine and ten last night?'

'I cannot say. I do not see why he need have been, but some of the Sergeant's affairs are curious, and I do not enquire into them.'

'You left Soho Square about eight o'clock, and I told you then that I meant to question a person known as Limping Mick today. Did you repeat that to Sergeant Clancy, and if so, at what time?'

'I did not. Why should I? It did not seem to be of any interest, and the Sergeant did not return here from some business of his own until very late. Nor do I understand the drift of all these questions.'

'They have their purpose, ma'am,' I said. 'Now then, were Mr. Lampeter and the Sergeant on conversational terms outside of your elegant establishment?'

'I understand so. Mr. Lampeter found him entertaining. I believe he enjoyed his tales of the wars from India to Waterloo.'

'As I can well understand. So he could have disclosed some part of his suspicions or discoveries?'

'It's very likely. I've already told you, sir, I did not press the Sergeant. He is sometimes inclined to regard his affairs as exceedingly profound.'

'Whereas you're inclined to take 'em with a pinch of salt? Believe me, ma'am, this one's more than profound. And I fancy you came to that view yourself on Thursday night. What part did Sergeant Clancy play in those events?'

'I cannot say. He returned here about ten, deeply perturbed. He said that Mr. Lampeter had met with a misfortune, and something about treachery. As a result his own intentions were disarranged. You were bound to investigate now, and he proposed to contrive a meeting with you to learn, if he could, what you might have discovered.'

'And to put himself on the right side. But you're a jewel of a wife, ma'am, to allow your husband to content you with a half-told tale.'

She gave me a pitying smile. 'I have my own ways of learning all I wish to know, and in this I do not wish. I have my young ladies to think of. In my opinion the Sergeant is meddling in matters too deep for him.'

'He is indeed,' I observed. 'Now tell me, does the word "Cato" have any meaning for you? Has Clancy ever spoken of it?'

'Cato? It conveys nothing to me. Neither has the Sergeant ever mentioned it.'

'So consider these also—"*Delenda est Carthago.*" "When does the clock strike?" "Precisely on the hour." '

This time she gazed at me as if I had taken leave of my senses. 'To me they are mere gibberish.'

'They all have their significance. But we don't get much for'arder, ma'am, so I must talk with Clancy himself. Where is he?'

'Nor can I tell you that, I fear. He was out early this morning. I don't rise at that hour myself, and I have not seen him since.'

'Ma'am,' I advised her, 'I'm keeping my patience as best I can, but it's wearing threadbare. I'll leave a message for him. I shall be supping at Hackett's Eating House tonight. I shall expect him to present himself there, and he'll fail me at his peril. I daresay you've learned by now that I've been seconded to a higher authority than Bow Street, and in my new department we don't brook obstruction from anybody.'

'Mr. Sturrock,' replied she coolly, 'if you're seconded to Heaven, I still can't inform you of what I don't know. And don't wish to know.'

I moderated my tone a bit. 'Very well, ma'am. We understand each other, and I'll not detain you longer, but for two last matters. One not all that important, though I'm curious. When I was talking with Sergeant Clancy on Friday, he said that you had certain news for me concerning our meeting in Brussels long ago.'

She seemed relieved. 'At least I can answer that. And it might be in the nature of a warning. Do you recollect a young woman by the name of Polly Andrews? A bold, unbiddable creature.'

'Let me think now,' I said, casting my mind back. 'Why yes. At one time a lady's maid in Lady Dorothea Hookham-Dashwood's household. She was concerned in an abduction plot, and worse. I let her off light when she might have suffered for it, and placed her in your care to mend her manners.' *

'Quite so,' said Mrs. Clancy. 'But creatures of that

* *Suicide Most Foul.*

90

impudence are not always grateful for mercy. I was at pains to teach her better behaviour, and even took her with us when we went to Paris. Nevertheless, she left us there, and to be plain, I thought good riddance to bad baggage. However I saw her again here in London a few days ago; in Motley's Haberdashery. Dressed to the fashion, and seemingly well funded. I was not forthcoming with her, but she had the impertinence to observe, "I see you do very well, Mrs. Clancy, and so do I. And when you next see our mutual friend Mr. Jeremy Sturrock, pray tell him that I still have a score or two to settle." '

'So ho,' I announced, for in that instant a light of inspiration dawned on me; and maybe an even greater light, reflecting upon the woman Jagger had thought he knew the cut of at The Hog In The Pound. 'I'm profoundly obliged, ma'am,' I said.

'Then take care, sir. Such creatures can be spiteful. And as you've so delicately hinted,' the good lady added sweetly, 'Mr. Sergeant Clancy and I have need of you.'

'Likewise as I've already said, we understand each other. So now there's only one last question left, and very simple. Do you know of the late Mr. Lampeter's lodging?'

She paused a minute, but she knew it plain enough, and at last she said, 'If it will help to bring his murderers to book I think I might tell you. It's Portman Square, Number Fifty-Four. A most respectable address.'

'An exceedingly respectable address,' I agreed, seeing yet more light, but not much surprised. 'And with your permission, ma'am, I'll take leave of you on that.'

'So there we have it,' I said at the end of a long recital, when old Abel Makepenny, me and Maggsy were finishing our supper at Hackett's: a nice goose with trimmings, a pretty fair baked pie, and a round of Stilton. 'There's no doubt that Polly Andrews, Julia Bracegirdle, and the woman that Jagger caught sight of at The Hog are all one trollop.'

Abel took a deep draught of his port. Maggsy agreed, 'Looks like it,' and I went on, 'She's a small bit of the plot. It ain't common to have women conspirators, but we know she's mischievous by nature, and they're all getting notions above themselves these days. Her part was to get me in discredit at Bow Street so that I don't have proper support for investigation. These rascals're perfectly aware that I'm their greatest danger, and the Bracegirdle ploy was meant to gain 'em a few days grace. She's most likely a doxy to one of the villains, though not Lampeter, as he had other interests. But he fell in with the gang by reason of lodging at the same house, for we know there's another one there. The fellows you reported discussing and confabulating with him,' I added to Maggsy.

Abel observed, 'That's a rare tasty Stilton—chimes well with the port. But pray continue, Jer'my.'

'We don't know whether the riot in Oxford Street was fortuitous or not. I'd consider it was. It even interfered with their plans. They'd discovered very near too late that Lampeter meant to split on 'em, followed him with intent, and was delayed themselves by it. So the unfortunate fellow got as far as my door before they came up with him. And then they had to dispose of him quick.'

Abel belched roundly and took to the port once more. 'But what happened after you got there and found the feller? Demned disgraceful, shootin' at a man on his own doorstep.'

'That was the spur of necessity. We came on the scene too soon for their comfort, and the shooting was to warn us off.'

'And my oath it did,' announced Maggsy.

I silenced him with a look. 'Because they had to remove the body lest I should find some means to identify it. And I couldn't have done that if it had not been for his tobacco pouch. A singular occurrence,' I mused. 'I've never before had a mystery which hung upon a handful of tobacco.'

'Particular nice consideration,' Abel agreed.

'For the rest,' I finished, 'we want Clancy. It's certain that he or some of his men witnessed at least a part of the later events. And where the devil is he?' I demanded. 'He should have been here long since.'

'If he gets here at all,' Maggsy muttered. 'The way this lot goes about it he's very likely on his way to the mortuary himself by now.'

Abel gazed at him owlishly and shook his head at me. 'If he don't appear, Jer'my, what d'you propose? You're fighting this battle on yer own. Best let me report it to the Magistrate.'

'And give my own mystery over to Lord Jackass? Have him take the credit? I'll see him in hell first. I've several shots in my locker yet, besides Clancy. See now, Abel, today's Saturday. Give me tomorrow and Monday. If I don't get to the nub of it by then I'll come to Bow Street in person, and take my hat off to his lordship myself.'

'Begod,' he observed, 'I hope I may hear the conversation. Well enough, Jer'my. But if it is an assassination plot . . .'

'What else can it be?' I demanded. 'And Clancy spoke of the St. Peter's Fields rascal, Thistlewood, the other day.'

'That ranting villain.' Abel shook his head. 'You'd need an army to search for him in London. And you can be sure he's well hid.'

'I don't mean to try. We don't have time. We must find out what "Cato" means. But nobody I've flung the word at so far knows of it.'

'Marco Porcius Cato the Elder,' Abel recited. 'Better

known as Cato the Censor. Occupied all the ranks of the Roman Magistracy at one time or another, and set himself out to put down every kind of luxury and show when he was elected to Censor. A good worthy man no doubt, but must have been a damnation misery—and he had a bee in his bonnet about Carthage. Never stopped speechifying, and finished very near every speech he made with "Delenda est Carthago." '

'Quite so,' I said, somewhat nettled with the old gentleman for trying to instruct me in my history. 'Carthage should, or must be, destroyed. It's a political utterance of demagogues. So change the word "Carthage" to whatever you're conspiring against these days—or even *who*ever.'

'Aye,' Abel answered profoundly, 'I take your drift,' while I continued, 'These conspirators must needs always to do their business in terms of Drury Lane melodrama and match their cant to the occasion. That's why they're so damned dangerous. Plain, simple words ain't good enough for 'em. They reckon themselves as actors of Destiny on an heroic stage, and as such they ain't aiming at any common Tom or Dick. True enough they've murdered a few common poor devils so far, but that's by the way. The last act's yet to come. "When does the clock strike." It's as plain as your nose that "strike" is the word of meaning—the act itself, and not unlikely with further inference of the end of one period and the start of another. "Precisely on the hour if it keeps good time." And to me that sounds as if the time is already decided, which argues that so also is the place. And the person.'

'Begod,' Abel breathed. 'Yer drift's plain enough, Jer'my.' He looked all about mysteriously, much as if he were a conspirator himself. 'A certain fat Gentleman?' he whispered with a sort of fearful joy.

'No names,' I said. 'But there's a lot points that way.'

'Aye.' He took another deep draught of port while considering it. 'That might well be your villains' Carthage—him and his antics. And Rome was a republic when that old pest Cato was making his demned long-winded speeches. Is that what you reckon they're after? A republic?'

'Thistlewood and others have said it often enough. And they ain't alone. They've got the open support of some considerable families—the Hamiltons and Graftons, to name but two. And there's no respect for the monarchy now.'

'The Whigs . . .' He gave a remarkable sniff. 'But I'll grant it looks like it. Yet I dunno. *Assassination*, Jer'my. It ain't well thought of here. It'd set the people they most need against 'em from the start.'

'Abel,' I said, 'in the Midlands and North they're bands already drilling and sharpening blades and pikes. It's well known. I've heard the situation in those parts described as much what it was like in Massachusetts in seventy-three. American notions are damnation catching.'

'Maybe. But in so doing they're fast frightening off the middle sort of folk they must have to support 'em. Orator Hunt might get the mobs roaring and cheering after him, but one wild speech of his does more for Liverpool's government than all their new Acts of Parliament. Nonetheless . . .' He seemed to fall into a comfortable port wine and academic reflection on a Royal assassination and its consequences. '. . . The succession's straightforward enough,' he mused. 'It'd go to William of Clarence. "Silly Billy" they call him, but he's amiable and a sailor, he'd be acceptable. Or there's some who might speak for Kent's daughter, young Victoria. But she's a mere babe yet, and that'd mean another Regency. And I don't just see her mother, Victoria of Saxe-Coburg . . .' He sniffed again. 'Moreover, Wellington's on hand,

and a Tory, and within an hour of the event he'd be put in charge of public order. He wouldn't stand no nonsense.' He shook his head. 'It's a nice speculation, Jer'my, but I'd say . . .'

'Abel,' I commanded him sharply, 'wake up.' He came to with a start, and I continued, 'The King ain't the only pebble on the beach. To be sure he looks the most likely, but I've got another gentleman stuck fast in my mind. In short, Lord Harrowby.'

'Harrowby?' Abel repeated, staring at me as if I were out of my wits. 'God's sake, why? He's nobody, not compared with the King. You take the most uncommon fantastical notions now and again, Jer'my. True enough he's a great Officer of State, Lord President of the Council, but that don't mean a lot. If he fell dead on this instant there'd be another appointed tomorrow with never a ripple, and nobody a ha'porth the better or worse off. I don't see the *point* of thet notion, Jer'my.' And he was clearly peevish at the thought of it. 'I doubt there's more'n one in a thousand of your malcontents ever heard his name or knows what his office is. God's sake, what's took your fancy that way?'

'I don't know,' I confessed. 'But there's sublety here, Abel. Whoever these villains may be, Thistlewood or not, or around him, they've got a clear plan devised.' I recounted the incident of Jagger recognising the man, Bragg, in The Hog In The Pound and finished, 'Don't ask me why, for I can't tell you. But I've a sure instinct. I'm certain we've a thread there if we can pick it up. And what I want from you, Abel, is all the information you can discover about his lordship. Where he lives, town house and country seat, where he's in residence now, what he's doing, and all he's appointed to do in the next week or so.'

'Be damned,' Abel protested, turning very near as sulky as Maggsy gets now and again, 'you give your orders, don't you? For what it's worth, his town house's in Grosvenor Square, but you ain't asking much for the rest. What in damnation do you take me for?'

'An uncommon expert who knows more about the doings of the nobility than any ten of the rest of us put together,' I told him cunningly. 'You're better placed for the job than I am, Abel, and shrewder at it. So be a good fellow now. I want that information, and I want it quick.'

'You're supposin' ahead of yer facts again,' he complained. 'You'll do best to keep the King in consideration. A fine fool you'll look if he gets himself assassinated while you're off roaring after mere Harrowbys and suchlike.' Nevertheless he was considerably mollified, and at last he grumbled, 'But I can see I must do what I can for yer.'

By this time it was near half past ten, and very clear that if Abel kept at the port much longer somebody would have to take him back to his lodging, as well as the risk of him forgetting what I wanted from the condition of his head in the morning. I said, 'We can't get much for'arder now. We've done pretty well, and it's about time to adjourn. But where the devil is Clancy?'

'I've told you once,' Maggsy answered, sober but sour. 'On his way to the mortuary. If he ain't there already.'

'Confound your miseries,' I started, but even as I spoke I perceived a fellow conferring with one of the serving men, looking about the settles as if in search of somebody; half seen at first in the tobacco smoke and fog and lamplight, but as he approached resolving into the man who had admitted me to Panton Street that afternoon. Before he addressed me I had a premonition of what his presence foretold. 'Mr. Sturrock, sir,' he said, taking a folded paper from his hat, 'begging your pardon, but this here special and in haste from Mrs. Clancy.'

Nor need I relate what it contained. It was brief and plain: *Mr. Sturrock. Sir: I beg to inform you that it had not*

*proved possible to deliver your message to Mr. Sergeant Clancy,
as at this time—viz. ten o'clock—he has not returned altho'
expected here by particular arrangement not later than seven. In
consideration of your several disclosures, etc., today I must
request your forebearance, and express the obligation for your
interest and attention, of, with respect, Mrs. B. Clancy.*

I digested this in silence, and with heartfelt restraint
refrained from expressing any observations. But I looked
curiously at Master Maggsy. 'I begin to suspect,' I said,
'that you are now starting to add the gift of prophecy to
all your other horrible attributes.'

— 7 —

So THERE WE have the situation at half of the hour past ten on Saturday night, February 19, and despite my bold words to Abel I was profoundly perturbed. But there was no virtue in confessing it, for a good general must always seem to be in command of his strategy, and I began even to perceive a certain advantage in this latest baulk. I had said often enough that I could do with half a dozen more men, and here was an excellent opportunity to get 'em. I set about issuing my orders, quick and sharp.

'Very good,' I said to the Panton Street fellow. 'I want you now to return to Mrs. Clancy as quick as you can. Do a Wellington Quick Step.' This being the famous rapid march of one hundred paces walking and one hundred trotting, with which the Duke moved his forward regiments at disconcerting speeds in Spain. 'Tell Mrs. Clancy,' I continued, 'that I am giving the matter my most urgent and immediate attention. But inform her that I shall require the loan of her carriage, the service of Corporal Pikestaff, and as many of Sergeant Clancy's men as can be mustered at short notice. They are all to understand that they are under my absolute command, and they are to report to my chambers, ready for action, within the hour. Is that plain?' The man seemed somewhat dubious about absolute command, but I said, 'I see it is. So you may finish the rest of the port here to refresh yourself, and then be off.' There was barely more than a mouthful of it left.

'If he gets there without his head knocked,' Maggsy observed, but I did not trouble myself to answer him, and turned next to Abel. That foolish befuddled old gentleman was still musing about the intricacies of the Succession between the Dukes of Clarence and Kent should His Majesty George Fourth unfortunately be lost to us, but I said, 'Come now, Abel. I've curious work afoot tonight, and it's time you were out of harm's way in your bed.'

'Dunno about Victoria, Jer'my,' he muttered. 'A mere babe yet, and nobody'd accept a Saxe-Coburger as Regent; nor I dunno how the Commons'd take to another Queen. Poor Queen Anne never did herself nor nobody else a wonderful lot of good. It'll have to be Silly Billy.'

'Abel,' I said, 'with all due respect and reverence, be damned to the Duke of Clarence. Wake yourself up. Get off and find a hackney, Maggsy, we'll go with him. And Abel,' I finished, 'on your life and peril don't forget that I want a full report of all Lord Harrowby's appointments for the next week or so.'

'God's whiskers, you can't mean to go looking for him tonight,' Maggsy protested as our dreadful bone-shaking conveyance rattled us back into the square, having first deposited Abel at his lodging and seen him safe inside. 'Hunting for a pin in an haystack,' the wretch persisted. 'An' an haystack in a bloody fog as well.' For the fog was indeed thickening again.

'A promise to a lady is a pledge to be kept at any inconvenience,' I said, while dismounting to pay off our surly dog of a driver, with the usual London compliments on either side. 'Whether we find the rascal or not, dead or alive, may be another matter, but a gentleman must always show willing. Besides, I've bargained for a certain advantage. And begod, here it is already,' I added, for just as our first cranky flea-trap trundled away into the dark, still with blessings floating back on the mist, a better kind of carriage pulled into the square and came round to us at a brisk military clip. 'How is it that these hackney scoundrels must always be so vulgar?' I demanded of the air, and then enquired 'Is that you, Corporal Pikestaff?'

'Present,' he barked. 'And a detail of six men. To stand by for instructions.'

'Very good,' I replied in the same smart style. 'Then follow me to receive 'em.'

If the fellow chose to play soldiers there was no harm in humouring him, and I led the way at a sharp pace indoors and up to our sitting room; there surprising Master Jagger, who was smoking like a lord, reclining in my best chair with his feet up on another, and the Madeira close handy at his elbow. 'God help us,' he cried, 'I thought it was a herd of elephants tramping up the stairs,' while Maggsy gave his wicked snigger, but I said, 'Don't disturb yourself now, you're still a sick man,' and turned from him to survey my curious force.

And a precious hard tack lot they looked; respectable enough as to attire and general tidiness, very near a parade turn out, but otherwise a villainous wooden-faced crew. They would serve my purpose very well, and I was properly thankful for the cleverness on Clancy's part which had given them to me, for I suspected now that he considered himself uncommon clever—unless the poor fellow had indeed met with some misfortune.

'As fine a body of men as I've ever seen,' I observed. 'And you all know what we're here for. Your respected Sergeant's reported missing, and it's our business to find him. We may do it tonight if we're fortunate, or it might take us tomorrow or even a day or two, for London's an uncertain place these days. But first of all we must find out where to start. So when was he last seen?'

'About ten of the forenoon today,' Pikestaff snapped briskly.

I nodded. 'Very good. That's the sort of short answer I like. And what were his instructions at ten o'clock today?'

'Same as yesterday. Standing orders.'

'As might be expected. But let's go back a bit. Was the Sergeant, or any of you men, or any others of the platoon, in or close by Watkins' Yard in Long Acre last night?'

A row of wooden faces, never a blink, until Pikestaff answered, 'Not as I knows to. Wasn't no brief to that effect.'

'Quite so. And what were your standing orders?'

'General duties as required by Mrs. Sergeant,' Pikestaff recited. 'The detail as before to escort you.'

'Ah yes. I recollect. But now then, when last seen today, did the Sergeant give any hint of what business he was about, or where he was going? And did any other man go with him?'

'Went alone. Nor didn't communicate with his intentions. It ain't his habit unless we're instructed to rondeyvous.'

'Beggin' your pardon, Corporal,' one of the others broke in, and I now perceived the amiable Private Potter, who had so much admired my fighting style today. 'Beggin' your pardon, but I could have swore he says he was going to Marylebone.'

'Speak when you're spoken to, Potter,' snarled the Corporal. 'But true, come to think of it, sir. It slipped my mem'ry. It was a household commission for Mrs. Sergeant, as had cause to complain of goods delivered by a certain hemporium.'

'Very proper,' I agreed. 'Some of these tradesmen will deliver anything if they get the chance. But I hope there's nothing else slipped your memory, Corporal. What was the name of this emporium?'

'Wasn't informed, sir. Private Potter must've heard of it listening to orders that didn't concern him. Which I've had occasion to charge him on before.'

'It's unfortunate,' I said. 'We might've had somewhere to jump off from. Though the place will be shut up at this time of night anyway. So we must start elsewhere. I want two men detailed to the St. Giles Mortuary, Corporal Pikestaff.'

'Very good,' said he without an expression on the oaken face. 'Privates Potter and Gage—one pace forward.'

'The mortewry?' repeated Private Potter, while Maggsy gazed at me plainly wondering what the devil I was about now, but I continued kindly to Potter, 'Where you fell in after me this morning. If the worst has already happened, though we may pray it hasn't, that's the place we shall hear of it quickest. The custodian there is a fellow named Gotobed, and that is where he's most likely to be at this hour if he's not browsing in his Bible. Either way you're to rouse him up and keep him awake and waiting until you receive further instructions.'

'Asking pardon,' said the man, Gage, 'I don't rightly understand these orders,' and Maggsy muttered, 'I'm damned if I do neither.'

'It's clear and simple,' I told them. 'If the Sergeant's already there it's no more than your duty and respect to sit there with him for a bit. Or if he's not you'll find Gotobed a cheerful fellow. You can exchange tales with him—yours of Waterloo or his about Trafalgar. But in either case you'll remain at the mortuary until relieved.'

'Any further questions?' demanded the Corporal. 'No time for 'em. So quick march.'

There was a certain air of nonplussment as this first

pair left, but I did not offer any explanation, and turned next to Jagger. 'Now my lad, you can stir your wits. You spoke of a rascal named Bragg today. Is he likely to be at The Hog In The Pound at this time of night? And if he is, what does he look like? Is there any way we can pick him out without asking for him by name?'

'He might be, and you might do,' Jagger replied, somewhat sulky. 'Very near lives there, so far as I know. Works potman for his beer and vittles, and sleeps in the stable when he can't wheedle a woman to give him lodging. You'll know him plain enough, as he's got a scar down the left-hand side of his chaps and one eye half closed. Got it from a knuckle duster in a discussion after a cock fight.'

'Evidently a villainous looking fellow. You men will note that description,' I said, and went on to give them their full instructions. 'I shall follow with Maggsy in the carriage, Corporal Pikestaff driving,' I finished. 'When we arrive, wait for me to give the nod, and then let it all be done quiet and orderly if you can.'

'Description noted, and orders clear,' barked Pikestaff. 'Get fell in, you four. Quick step all the way.'

'And me,' Jagger announced. 'If you're going to stir up The Hog, so am I. I got a reckoning of my own to settle there.'

'I don't mean to stir up anything more than we must,' I told him. 'It'll all be calm and peaceful, and I don't want you getting quarrelsome. You'll stay where you are. You might not know it, but you're dead. You died last night.'

'Calm and peaceful,' Maggsy observed bitterly when we were in the carriage and on our way. 'With you and that lot of villains? My oath, it looks like calm and peaceful. I don't see what you're getting at anyway.'

'Another shot at random,' I told him. 'Or you might say dropping a cannon ball into the water to see what comes up. With Clancy seemingly lost to us now, we must find information any way we can. We're still getting it only in bits and snippets. There's twice today I've heard Marylebone mentioned.'

'What d'you mean,' he demanded, '*seemingly* lost to us? Is he or ain't he? Is he in that mortuary by now, or not?'

'I doubt it,' I said. 'The mortuary's merely part of my plan. And keep your horrid voice down—we don't know how much Pikestaff can hear up there on the box. Otherwise use your wits. Clancy's no more disappeared or met with misfortune that I have. The rascal's lying low at Panton Street. I'll own that I was taken in for a bit, but I'm damned certain now that he's still frying his own fish, with or without Mrs. Clancy's aid and encouragement. He's too much of an old soldier to get himself caught like Mr. Lampeter or Tomlin's boy and Limping Mick. It's plain he don't mean to tell what he knows yet, and that tale of disappearing's a mere subterfuge. It suits me well enough for the present. Clancy can wait awhile, for I've got the best of the bargain—six men and a carriage on the pretext of showing concern and looking for him.'

The wretch uttered his disagreeable sniff. 'If you ask me, all you've got is a damnation lot more complexication. And what's Marylebone got to do with it?'

'It's another of the snippets. Jagger heard it mentioned just before he was struck down the other day. You heard simple Private Perkins blurt out that that's where Clancy was going this morning. Think it out for yourself. If you don't see it, I don't have time to explain,' I said, for we were then coming up to The Hog. It was on the late side for respectable people, but the place was still open and even doing a fair business. Despite the fog there was the usual gang of vulgar idlers loitering outside, several horses, and a flash town phaeton—evidently some young sporting blood—and Bully Wheeler's own private conveyance in the yard: an old mail coach which he had bought cheap and refurbished for driving uncommonly select parties to race meetings and other events. Torches and lanterns, and a shifting light in the darkness, but nobody seemed to take much note of us except one of our men already stationed in the doorway. This fellow took off his beaver to wipe round inside it with a bandanna, and I said, 'They're in position, Corporal. Turn your cattle round so you'll get a quick clear start when we leave—have one of these rascals stand by 'em, and then come in after us.'

'And for God's sake keep it peaceful, like you said,' Master Maggsy entreated behind me as we made our way inside.

'I've none but the most pacific intentions,' I assured him, surveying the company.

It was a rare London mix; from the common horse dung to the pretended bloodstock. An air very near as thick as the fog outside, but stinking different, a haze of lamplight, faces of various villainy, and such a general picture as Hogarth himself might have depicted in his more critical or despondent mood. Stablemen and grooms, no doubt from the new residential squares nearby; persons of better attire, though of vulgar and dubious appearance; one rascal who was dressed as a parson if my eyes did not deceive me, which would have been easy enough in that smoke; Bully Wheeler resplendent in his own special corner, with four or five Dandies or Corinthians, all dressed to an extravagance of fashion. And our own old soldiers not a lot better looking than any of the rest of the motley crowd here.

Our arrival again went without notice for a minute, time enough for one of the platoon to edge past me and murmur, 'Your man's marked, yonder by the yard door,' and for me to reply, 'Surround him there then, and remove him that way.' Then Pikestaff was behind, adding, 'Wait for the order,' with Master Maggsy also muttering another prayer, as on that instant Wheeler caught sight of me, and cried 'God's whips!' in the bluff, old fashioned coaching manner he always affected when consorting with the Dandies. 'Here's an unexpected honour.'

I said nothing, for our men were then working round through the press to the fellow, Bragg, but one of the Dandies turned to survey me through a quizzing glass, an apparition with rouge on his face and a stock so high that it very near pushed his head backwards. 'Eged, Wheelah,' he enquired, 'what's this? A bookmaker's jumper come to dun yer? The fellah looks most confounded like one.'

'Oh my God,' whispered Maggsy, but with one eye on our men I held my fire, and Wheeler answered, 'Odd's Blood, no, Sir Clipsley. You'll offend the gentleman. This is the famous Mr. Sturrock of Bow Street—or was late of Bow Street.'

'A Wobin Wedbreast?' said the painted popinjay; this being the jeering name by which the old Bow Street Runners were once known. He raised his quizzing glass at me once again. 'Weally, I'm demned. I never set eyes on one before.'

'Then take care you never set eyes on one once too often, sir,' I advised him, 'or you might well be damned. I've no concern with you, or not yet. My business here is with Mr. Wheeler. And that,' I said, 'is a matter of assault and murder.'

You could have heard a pin drop in the sudden hush. One and all of the rascals had been grinning like dogs in anticipation of a rare bit of bear baiting, but that word struck 'em all dumb. Every pair of eyes in the house was on me through the smoke, with such pallid and gobble chap looks as by now would have given even Hogarth the cold grues. It was coming up close for my signal, for by this our men were well placed about Bragg, but I said aside to Pikestaff, 'Let 'em hold for another minute,' and continued, 'In a case of murder, Mr. Wheeler, *late* of Bow Street don't signify. I can lay an information against you as accessory before the fact.'

'You can what?' he demanded with several additions, forgetting his Dandy affectations. 'That be damned, and you. What the devil d'you mean? There's never been no murder in my house.'

'Quite so,' said I, still in the same strange hush. 'Those were near enough the very words you used on Thursday last. I've no doubt you recollect the occasion. A man by the name of Jagger, who asked some nonsense catchword doggerel that's being bandied about in every ale house and tavern in Long Acre and Covent Garden.' I noted that one of the better-dressed sort glanced sideways at another, though not the Dandies, who were staring open-mouthed, and I added, 'What it may mean I neither know nor care. I've no time to fret with nursery riddles. But Jagger was struck down. You are known to have cried out, "Not in my house," Mr. Wheeler, and some other person then present said something about Marylebone, to the effect of "take him to Marylebone".' I looked all round the villain's gallery of horrid faces. 'Which is what I want to know. Where in Marylebone was this man carried off to and done to death?'

And on that instant the fracas fell upon us, although I am still uncertain precisely how it began. Maggsy declared afterwards that some rascal behind struck at me with a pot, and that he warded it off. Pikestaff said that another raised a cudgel, which he caught at. But Wheeler started, 'I don't know nor care, the man was quarrelsome,' while the Dandy he called Sir Clipsley cried, 'Thwow the wude fellow out, Wheelah, he's not pwopah company.' Whereupon one of the other fops negligently tossed a mug of beer at me, and it may not be unlikely that I caused some further confusion myself by heartily snouting him in return. But whatever it might have been, all was uproar in an instant.

The lower sort of London taverns are frequently riotous, for some of the liquors they dispense are an incitement to violence, but never have I seen a mill like this. I barely had time to cry, 'On your orders,' before I was beset by half a dozen. Nevertheless I gave myself the pleasure of tapping Sir Clipsley's claret for him first, for I had taken a curious dislike to the gentleman. He went down into a welter of arms and legs with an affronted squeal, though whether for his somewhat crushed nose, his spattered stock, or his offended dignity I could not say, and I turned my attention to the others. Another scoundrel came at me with a broken bottle, which I disapproved of and crowned him with a quart pot, then tossed one more over the counter, while Master Maggsy laid about wicked and reckless with a broken chair leg.

Mr. Bully Wheeler was now on all fours under a table, bellowing like a cow in calf for the watchmen and militias. Sir Clipsley was trying vainly to staunch his claret and crying, 'Assault and battewy,' in doleful accents. Clouds of dust rising in the smoke, a serving wench screeching rape and murder above the general observations, Master Maggsy adding his own unlovely chorus, and Corporal Pikestaff cursing wonderfully as he caught two rascals each by the scruff and knocked their heads together. 'Out of this,' he barked at me. 'They've got your man. Time to retreat.'

Retreat was easier said than done however, for by this time it was a pretty fair battle royal between ourselves and the door. I disposed of two more to clear a path as Master Maggsy bawled, 'Watch your back!' and struck another down behind me. I then seized a stool myself to batter our way through willy-nilly, and was just about to do fearful execution with it when a voice of authority rose clear above the uproar. 'Quiet, you dogs!' it cried with such command that there was a sudden strange hush. Even I was arrested by it, and I turned to perceive one more of the Dandies; this one a fellow of very different calibre from the unfortunate Sir Clipsley. In short a particular cool specimen of your true sporting Corinthian, as lean as a whippet and a look about him as if he cared nothing for either man or devil; in build and manner much resembling my very good old friend Sir Tobias Westleigh as that famous sportsman had been in his younger days.

'Stand aside, all of yer,' said he in the same tone of command, advancing unhurriedly through the litter of stools and tables, just as unhurriedly divesting himself of his elegant coat and tossing it negligently to one of the others. 'You stand in need of a sharp lesson, my fine bullfinch,' he added to me. 'Put your mauleys up, if you dare. Or shall I set this rabble on you again?'

'God's sake come out of it,' Maggsy begged. 'You know his sort. He'll make pig's pudden out of you.'

I answered the wretch as he deserved, but measured the distance to the door with my eye for a fighting withdrawal. 'Fall back behind me,' I told Pikestaff softly, and then cried, 'Why, sir, willingly, if that's your fancy. But no kicking or gouging. We'll fight by the Broughton Prize Ring Rules, and I'll warn you that I've stood my dozen rounds or more with Gentleman Jack before now.' This Gentleman Jack being a much admired and most artistic pugilist.

'Have you, by God?' said he, with an easy laugh. 'Well then, Jack's a rare old crony of mine. So we'll see how many rounds you may stand with me. You may have your bullfinch to pluck his feathers when I'm done with him,' he promised the ugly crowd all about us; so began the most notable bout of fisticuffs I have ever indulged in. It was like trying to hit quicksilver, for the man was very near as skilled as I am, and a perfect dancing master on his feet. He came in fast and low to start with and I gave ground a bit towards the door, to the jeers of the mob. Next he tried a cunning right-hand pass to cover a pile-driver left which might have floored me incontinent had I not stepped back in time, opened my guard to encourage him, and replied ding-dong with a trick or two of my own. That steadied the good fellow for a breath-less minute, and we fell to feint and jab, cut, parry, and hook for a brief but lively exchange—as pretty an exhibi-tion fight as any of the undeserving rascals here had ever been privileged to witness—though by now they were one and all baying for blood.

My tactics was very simple. To hold him at reach for a bit while watching that wicked left, fall away towards the door before opening to let him come on again, stop him with another head ringer or two, and then out before the mob had time to move, for I had no doubt of what they would do once I went down. All easy enough, and all had to be done in good order but for the confounded man changing his own style of a sudden. Throwing aside every pretence of science he came in like a bull, clearly meaning close fighting, which I much disapprove of. I stopped him for a minute with one, and two, and then three short arm-jabs, but he was not to be discouraged; he hammered in still closer, and even damned near got his left arm around my neck, while the rabble howled like wolves. And then, under cover of the horrid chorus, he said in my ear, 'Easy, be damned to you, and listen. Look for Inge, the butcher.' That was close on my undoing, for I dropped my guard in surprise, and he came up with a dirty clip to the jaw which might have felled a lesser man. 'Must keep this scum entertained, they'll kill you else,' said he with another light laugh, then drew away once more. And this time I must perforce close in myself, for I wanted more now, and meant to have it. 'God's sake, break it,' Maggsy implored from behind, 'get back to the door,' but I closed regardless of retreat, and then followed this curious conversation between feints and dodges and blows.

'Who is this Inge, and where is he?' A further cut at my chin, which I parried and answered with a lively right hook. A gasp, and, 'Damn and blast you for that, I could lay you cold if I tried. I'm but toying with you, Bullfinch—the name Inge, and that's all, can't tell you no more, I don't know.' A jab to the ribs which half winded me, but I got out, 'Confound you, sir, who are you and what's your interest?' I gave him one back to even the score, but he replied with a fresh laugh and added, 'You'll be a fair boxer some day if you live long enough, and no more questions, Master Bullfinch—I'm away to the country tomorrow, out of the trouble that's coming.'

'Be damned, sir,' I started, jerking off again from his wicked left. 'Did you know a man called Lampeter?' I demanded, and rattled his head for him. 'Aye,' he answered between his teeth. 'A good fellow, and I said no more questions.'

Whereupon he came at me like a whirlwind, cut, smash, and jab, while the mob howled a pandemonium for the kill. It was a matter of mere defensive fighting, for I have never seen a man so fast. Moreover I was nice about not inflicting a too-severe punishment on the sporting gentleman, as I now perceived that he had used our private bout as a clever means of passing information. In short, I was too nice by half, and the scoundrel took dastardly advantage of my kindness. I let him drive me back near enough to the door, then started politely, 'I'm profoundly obliged, sir . . .' but was cut short by a drayman's salute which lifted me clean in the air and into the waiting arms of Maggsy and Corporal Pikestaff.

'Be damned, what hit me?' I demanded, finding myself hustled across the yard towards our carriage, and Master

Maggsy replied, 'A blacksmith's sledgehammer by the way you sailed. You met your match that time,' he added with evil satisfaction.

'And be damned to that also,' I retorted, gathering my wits. 'I allowed the fellow to do it. Where's Bragg?'

'Trussed up and in the kerridge,' snarled Pikestaff. 'And in you get as well. We'd best sod off out've this before that lot catches us.' For the mob was already bursting out through the door and baying after us like a mad menagerie.

'Very good,' said I, taking command once more. 'So we now proceed to the St. Giles Mortuary; and you may go as fast as you like.'

—8—

SOMEWHAT TO MY displeasure, two of our platoon were
already in the carriage with Bragg, while seemingly the
others were getting up on the box with Corporal Pikestaff, thus sadly overloading the vehicle. There was no
time for rearrangement however, as a swarm of the
rabble was already at our wheels threatening our lives
and doing their best to overturn us. Indeed for a minute
or two it looked like another battle, until the resourceful
Corporal made fine and free with his whip and somehow
got us off with a fearful lurch and bone-shaking clatter.

Then at last, when we had left the various imprecations, catcalls, missiles, etc., safely behind us, I had
leisure to survey our capture, what little could be seen of
him in the dark. A miserable specimen he was—a mere
dunghill crowster, fancying himself a gamecock but now
discovering he was plucked and trussed and ready for the
oven. 'So you're Bragg,' I observed kindly.

The rascal replied with a stream of harnessroom epithets, and one of our men growled, 'Stow that, cully, or
we'll stow it for yer. D'ye want him to talk plain,
guv'nor?' he asked.

'Not yet,' I said, for I had no slightest intention of
letting any of Clancy's men overhear my questions or his
answers. 'There's plenty of time. The poor fellow will
talk plain enough before I've done with him tonight.'

'Rot yer guts,' Master Bragg started, embarking upon

another flood of picturesque poesy until it was cut short by a soft thump and ended in a hollow belch. After that we proceeded in amiable silence for a time—though crawling lopsided and crabwise with the weight we had aboard—before the other man ventured, 'That was an uncommon sporting mill you put up, Colonel.'

'Pretty fair,' I agreed modestly. 'A nice strategic diversion. It gave you time to take this fellow unnoticed. Nobody will ever know what's happened to him now. If he's missed at all.'

'God damn . . .' Bragg started again in terror, and was once more pacified, while my new admirer continued, 'Nonetheless it ain't many as'd take on Lord Auberon Falconer, let alone stand up to him as long as that.'

'I like a good, scientific match,' I said, giving Master Maggsy a sharp jerk with my elbow as he emitted a curious snort. 'So you know the gentleman?'

The good man was decently bashful. 'I wouldn't say to speak to. But knows of him. A most oncommon sportsman. It's reckoned that if he warn't Nobility but took to the prize ring he c'd beat all comers. Carries a good bat at cricket as well, and rides his own hosses at Newmarket. And a rare fast whip. Drove the Bath Flyer once for a wager, and broke the best time with'n.'

'Indeed, who don't know of him?' I asked. 'My own coachman professes a special respect for his lordship. It's a pleasure to reflect that we've still got a few like him left to us, and that the best of 'em may be seen freely by all at The Hog. Who does Sergeant Clancy meet there?'

'Nobody partic'lar,' the other man answered quick and sharpish. 'You can come upon all sorts who'll tip you what's what if you ask the right way. He likes to lay out a sov'rin or two now and agen, and reckons to learn the odds first.'

'And very wise,' I observed warmly. 'There's no quicker way to the Fleet Prison than laying out your

116

money without proper information. So let's hope he's still with us to lay out another sovereign or two when the fancy takes him.'

Thereafter our man seemed disinclined for further conversation, and I was quite content to remain silent myself, for I had much to consider. Not least our noble pugilist leaving for the country tomorrow out of the trouble to come, and that cryptic advice, 'Find the butcher, Inge.' Someday, I resolved, I would meet Lord Auberon Falconer again, though not yet. He had made it plain enough that further enquiry would not be welcome, and it does not do to be too importunate with the sporting nobility. For the present I had several simpler and smaller fish to fry.

The first being Master Bragg; with the cells at Bow Street now denied to me, the St. Giles Mortuary was as good a place as any to keep him cool for the night, and put him in a mood for penitence and confession. 'Bring him in, but keep him secure,' I ordered when at last we arrived, and led the strange procession into Jonah Gotobed's sanctum—where we discovered him and Privates Potter and Gage deep immersed in reminiscence and small beer. A pretty scene in the lamplight, with a nice little fire burning, and Jonah holding forth about the old *Victory* and how him and Lord Nelson sailed clear through the French line of battle. He broke off at our entrance to cry his regular greeting, 'Here's a privilege again, Mr. Sturrock, though a late hour . . .' but then stopped on a breath at the spectacle of Corporal Pikestaff and our villains carrying Bragg like a sack of oats. 'Begod,' he said in some astonishment.

'A simple matter, Jonah,' I explained. 'We don't need no discussion. I want you to find this poor fellow a bed for the night.'

'A bed?' he repeated, while I continued, 'But we'll

have first things first. I've no doubt these men told you their business. We're seeking a certain Sergeant Clancy. You ain't got him here, I hope?'

'I has not, sir,' he replied. 'As I've already hinformed the gentlemen. Nothing fresh at all since your last henquiry. But . . .' He stopped again, scratching his head and gazing from me to Bragg. 'Did you say a *bed?*'

'Nothing fanciful,' I said. 'He don't expect sheets and lavender. One of your slabs in the storeroom'll suit him well enough.'

'One of my slabs? But . . .' He rolled his eye at Bragg once more. 'But he ain't entitled to a slab. He ain't *dead!* Nor likewise I can't enter him in my books. It's all against the regulations.'

Master Bragg added several fresh observations, and when he paused for breath I said, 'To be sure he's not, or not yet. But be damned to your regulations, Jonah, we've no time for 'em. You'll do as you're told. Get your lantern and lead the way.'

When I take that tone nobody stops for further discussion, and it was all done in another minute, though even Maggsy looked at me somewhat sideways. A strange silence as they carried the fellow in and laid him on the slab amid the other still and shrouded figures in this unwholesome vault, and I grew a trifle irritated. I said, 'When they come to murdering simple shop boys I'm not particular what I do myself. Now be off, all of you. You may dismiss your men, Corporal Pikestaff, but you can wait for me in Gotobed's office in case I discover news of Sergeant Clancy.'

So arose another legend of Sturrock as I was left alone with our unhappy rascal in the sickly light of a single candle. The chill and the wavering shadows about the place were very near enough to give even me the grues, and he was quiet suddenly; a pallid look on him and more than fearful, but harder than I expected, glaring at me speechless like a rat in a corner. 'This place is too cold for Hell,' I observed, 'and it'll be worse before morning. Worse still if you lie here for another day or two, as you well might. For my part I don't mean to stay any longer than I must, and no more need you if you don't fancy it. A few simple questions and short answers, and you may have a better lodging.'

He told me what I could do with myself, an act at once impossible and indecent, and I continued, 'Come, my lad, that won't do. I'm offering a plain bargain. Turn King's evidence and save your neck, or keep your mouth shut and hang for it. If you don't freeze to death first among the present company. They're not the warmest of bedfellows.'

'I've slept colder before now,' he answered with a further flow of gutter courtesy. 'And there's more'n me'll hang before this week's out. You'll be one of 'em and, by God, I'll come to watch you swing. The time's come for change, when the mighty shall be cast down and trampled underfoot like the lilies of the field.'

'It's a ranting hedge-preacher as well. You've learned your choruses from Arthur Thistlewood and his like, have you? But tell me now, what information have you passed to this Thistlewood or other persons concerning Lord Harrowby?' He did not answer but gave me a startled look plain even in the wan light, and I said, 'Very good. You're a poor simple fool. You're more eloquent in your silence than in your filthy speech.'

'You're the fool, not me,' he retorted. 'I don't aim to get my throat slit.'

'Now who'd do that, I wonder?' I held the lantern close to watch him better. 'Would it be the butcher, Inge of Marylebone?'

The rascal's face gave him away again, and I added, 'It's a butcher's trade, ain't it? And you're easy meat. Nor there's not a lot you can tell me now that I don't already know. But one thing more, maybe; though it don't matter much. Who is the man known as "Cato?" He'll be the ringleader, no doubt. So is that Thistlewood?'

'Cato?' He gazed at me in open astonishment and then of a sudden broke into a wheeze of cracked laughter, fetching echoes like Bedlam back from the vault. For half a minute I could have fancied that the other silent inmates were stirring in surprise and sitting up to reprove us. 'Who's the man known as "Cato?" ' He very near choked himself with it. 'By God, you *are* the fool, master. You don't know as much as a parson in a whore shop. So sod yourself off, and be damned to you.'

'Well enough,' I said, for I had learned a bit more, and the charnel house chill of the place was already eating into my bones. 'I'll leave you to cool till the morning. You'll talk about Cato by then.'

'I'm obliged to your lordship,' he cried, wheezing with fresh laughter. 'I'm out of harm's way here, and I ain't fanciful. You find Mister Cato for yourself. And Butcher Inge's sack. And watch he don't get you into it,' he bawled after me, as I took the lantern and went out and locked the door after me.

When I returned to the office, Jonah was still babbling about his books and regulations, with Master Maggsy looking soulful—a sufficiently curious spectacle—and Corporal Pikestaff waiting like a gatepost. They all gazed at me expectantly as I went to warm myself by the fire, and for Pikestaff's benefit I announced, 'Well, for what it's worth, he don't seem to know anything about Sergeant Clancy, and there's little more we can do tonight.'

He remained wooden. If he knew anything himself he was not giving it away, but he barked, 'Permission to ask. He don't know, or he ain't telling?'

'A bit of each,' I answered. 'He knows plenty about

other matters, but I got very little out of him. He's harder than I thought he might be. Nevertheless he'll talk free enough by the morning.'

Both Maggsy and Jonah spoke out together, 'You don't mean to leave him there?' and I said, 'It's as good a place as any. He'll find it a bit cooling to the blood. Otherwise as Shakespeare observes, "The sleeping and the dead are but as pictures".' 'So they might be,' Maggsy muttered, 'but I reckon he never seen any like what's kept here.'

'I doubt if he did,' I agreed, and added, 'Be damned to your regulations, Jonah,' as Gotobed started a fresh babble. 'I'll relieve you of him tomorrow after he's told me all I mean to know, but he's in your charge now and you'll let him out of there at your peril. He's fearful of his masters in this ugly business, and he'll throttle you without a second thought to escape if you give him half a chance. So you be off to your bed and let him lie where he is. And we'll do the same,' I finished, watching Pikestaff and cutting short Jonah's fresh protestations. 'You may take us back to Soho Square, Corporal, and then dismiss yourself.'

'The very thought gives me the abdabs,' declared Maggsy, when we were safe back in our chambers, a glass or two of Madeira at hand for nightcaps, and Jagger listening entranced and pop-eyed to his recital of our night's adventures. 'Starts with a tasty little riot at The Hog, gets in a stand upper against this lordship Corinthian, and a fancy conversation in between the punches, escape from the mob by little more than the tails of our britches, and then to top it all claps this cove in the mortuary with a convocation of corpses for company. He's getting worse, Jaggs. We've seen some slim tricks of his before, but this one takes the cake.' He addressed himself to me again. 'And suppose your Master Bragg takes a fit or something happens to him in the night, which is very likely considering this lot, what d'you get out of him then?'

I was struck passing uneasy by the wretch's proclivity for unholy prophecy, but shook my head. 'He's safe enough. They don't know where he is. And we've got a fair bit from him already. He gave it away as easy as a kitten. First, it's plain that he has passed information of some kind concerning Lord Harrowby. Precisely what that was I mean to discover tomorrow, but we can be sure now that Harrowby's the prime target of the conspiracy. Though I'm damned if I can see why if, as old Abel Makepenny swears, he ain't all that important.'

'Second, it's also sure that the headquarters are in Marylebone. Bragg gave that away just as clear. Which is where we shall find this butcher, Inge. Whether a butcher by trade or inclination ain't so certain, as by the way Bragg bawled about him and some kind of sack I've the notion that he's a bloodthirsty villain. And the mention of the sack's an oddity as well. Yet as Lord Falconer spoke of the fellow he's a butcher by trade. So is he the tradesman Clancy went to Marylebone to look for? Either way it'll be easy enough to find him.'

'Not by me it won't,' Maggsy announced flatly. 'Butcher by trade or inclination is all the same to me.'

'I'll have a go if you like,' Jagger offered. 'I've still got a score to settle with somebody.'

'God forbid after your last exploit,' I said, and continued, 'But "Cato" still remains a mystery. Bragg laughed like Bedlam, and even recovered some of his confidence when I proposed that it was the conspiratorial name of the leader of the gang. But what the devil else can it be? That's the first question the fellow must answer tomorrow. And answer it he shall, for then we'll have the whole affair in our hands.'

'If it ain't too big for us to hold,' Maggsy observed sourly.

Jagger was cogitating profoundly, sucking at his pipe

and furrowing his brow, like a ploughed field, in unaccustomed thought. 'See now,' he said at last, 'I got a notion. You recollect what you was saying about that cove on our doorstep. About the other bits he says, and then when he come to this "Cato," you had the fancy that he was going to add something else but couldn't get it out.'

'Cato . . . something?' Maggsy asked. 'Cato . . . what?'

'I dunno,' Jagger confessed. 'S'pose it was a house? I knowed of a horse once called Cato Court. But I dunno why.'

Maggsy gave his obnoxious sniff. 'And you'd best stick to the horses, Jaggs. That's what you understand. Leave the reckoning to Sturrock and me.'

'That'll do,' I interposed, foreseeing dissension. 'There was to have been another word or more, but it might take a month of Sundays to hit on it, and Bragg will tell me quick enough after a night in cold company. So we'll be off to our rest and sleep on it now, for we've a busy day to come. Since we haven't yet found Sergeant Clancy, we've still got the carriage and his men at our call, and I've ordered Corporal Pikestaff to report here sharp and early. Seeing you've got your own clever way with stablemen, Jagger, I'll have you go to Watkins' Yard to make certain enquiries as I shall instruct you. And you may pay another visit to Portman Square, Maggsy. While I shall deal with Master Bragg, and after that proceed to Marylebone. So to our repose; we've done pretty well today.'

But I have observed before that Providence sometimes sees fit to turn cantankerous. Indeed before this doleful Sunday was out I could have fancied that He had deserted the righteous altogether and gone over to the other side. The day started with fog again, as thick as burned soup and stinking as bad. Maggsy and Jagger went off about their work unwillingly, and Pikestaff reported late, now like an evil tempered gatepost. Nor were his men much better. They seemed uneasy, even the amiable Private Potter, when I gave them their orders, to the effect that we were still seeking Sergeant Clancy.

'Marylebone,' I said. 'There's reason to believe we might hear word of him there. You can go in pairs if you please, but quarter the parish and don't spare your enquiries. And while you're about it take note of every butcher's shop or stall you may find.' So Pikestaff dismissed them, though with an air as if he and they all knew they were out on a fool's errand, and I added, 'Now Corporal, we'll go to St. Giles.'

And there came the next intimation of the unkindly disposition of Providence today. A disorder apparent even before I descended from the carriage. The mortuary van standing unattended in the yard, and a bare-ribbed horse drooping half out of its stable. The door to Jonah's office open, and his assistant and driver standing as vacant as an empty chamber pot, by turns scratching his head and pausing to listen to a strange mumble from within. 'You there,' I cried, hastening across to the fellow, 'what's amiss here?' and he answered. 'Dunno, master. Found'n tied up in a sack.'

'Found what, you blockhead?' I demanded, thrusting him aside and then stopping hard myself at the spectacle of disorder which met my eyes. The table overturned and a chair broken, Jonah's high desk flung on its side, his precious book and papers scattered on the floor. And Jonah himself, grotesquely clad in a long nightgown, cursing and praying and scrabbling about to gather them up. 'What the devil's this?' I roared, though it was all too clear on the instant. He peered round on his hands and one knee, his face much resembling a mistreated beef-steak, and I added, 'By God, Jonah, if you've let my man escape I'll have your guts for it.'

'A privilege, Mr. Sturrock, sir,' he muttered foolishly. 'I likes to oblige when I can. The place ain't jest so shipshape today as you might wish to see it, nor as to escape, sir, I dunno . . .'

But I did not wait for him. I hastened through to the vault, finding that door also swinging open; and one short glance was sufficient. For my man had indeed escaped. Or so a parson might have said. He had escaped everything in this life.

There are those who call me a hard man, and I have seen much of every sort of ugly wickedness, but there was that here which curdled even my stomach. Bragg was still bound hand and foot, lying on his back, though it appeared he must have struggled for a time. Apart from that I hope I may forget his face; as I hope I may forget my own brief vision of the unholy scene in the darkness of this place a few hours since. The other shrouded figures were still silent and undisturbed, but a rolled bundle of one of the rough canvas shrouds told its own tale, and I felt my bowels heave again at the sight of it. There was nothing more to do with this fellow, and nothing more to learn from him. I spared him one more look and turned away.

In the office now Jonah had got himself to a chair, and was gazing about him as bemused as an owl in daylight. The other man was still peering from the doorway, half-minded what to do, and I said sharply, 'Bestir yourself there, fetch my driver in,' and continued, 'Come now, Jonah, wake up. You're more confounded than hurt. A shipmate of Nelson should be made of sterner stuff. What happened here?'

'Aye,' he muttered. 'True enough, Mr. Sturrock. I rec'lect aboard the old *Victory* . . .'

'Jonah,' I said, 'be damned to the *Victory*. What happened?'

Shorn of his rambling, the tale was short and simple.

He had been awakened, at some hour of the night unknown, by knocking at the outer door and a voice crying that the Parish Watchman had need of him. Such calls, although uncommon, were not unknown. Half asleep, he had been unable to strike a light to his candle and had fumbled to open the door in the dark. Then had followed a brief struggle before he was struck down. Something was flung over his head, and he knew nothing more until discovered by his assistant, Jasper Spark, not long before my own arrival.

'Did you catch sight of anybody?' I enquired. 'How many was there?'

'What could I catch sight of? 'Twas as black as the Pit. Might've been one or two, but no more'n that. I was took by surprise. Though they didn't have it all their own way by the look of this.' The unhappy man was very near weeping. 'God help us, here's a mess. I likes to oblige, Mr. Sturrock, but I wish you'd take your trade somewhere else. I s'pose it was on account of what you brought here last night? I haven't dared so much as look in the vault yet.'

'It was,' I answered, 'and it's unfortunate. It's a murder as wicked as any I've ever seen. The villain smothered him with one of your own damned shrouds.'

Jonah shook his head at me. 'It's a lesson, Mr. Sturrock. There's never no good comes of breaking regulations.'

'Count yourself lucky. He might've done for you too, though it seems he's a particular rascal. He kills wicked, but no more than he must. Well, where's my driver?' I demanded, as the man, Spark, came back.

The oaf was still scratching. 'He says the hosses is restive. Reckons they can smell something they don't like, and he darsent leave 'em. I dunno,' he added. 'They don't look all that restive to me.'

'And by God so can I smell something that I don't

like,' I announced. 'So let's have your end of the tale. You found Gotobed here tied up in a sack. Let me see that as well.'

Neither told me any more, however. The tale was nothing; the sack merely a common oats or corn bag. Such things may be found tossed aside in any stable. 'So there we have very little,' I pronounced at last. 'It's a serious matter now, Jonah, and I'm bound to say that you've been uncommon careless.'

'God's truth,' he cried in a strange fury. '*Me* been uncommon careless!' but I silenced him quick, and sent his man off to tell Pikestaff that I'd be out in a minute. Then I continued, 'Listen careful now, Jonah. We can't afford any more mistakes. This is a dangerous affair, and I don't want any damned inquisitive coroner's questions yet. So you'll do as you're told. Go yourself and take the cords off that fellows arms and legs. Do whatever it is you do with your other clients, and set it down in your precious books that he was found dead in Oxford Street a bit after twelve last night. He was brought here by several Dandies, who set about you when you requested their names and then made off.'

'But . . .' he started, and I said, 'Jonah, my man, if things go on as awkward as this for only the next few days, or even hours, it won't matter a lot, anyhow. Nobody won't be fretting much about an extra corpse or two.'

So back to Corporal Pikestaff, who was waiting like a graven image on the box of the carriage. I noted that as the man Spark had observed, the horses seemed quiet enough, but Pikestaff offered neither remark nor question although Spark must have told him that something was amiss here. The fellow was either surly or a good soldier, not speaking until spoken to, and I added nothing else myself except, 'Very good, Corporal—we'll now proceed to The Cricket Club Tavern in the Edgeware Road.'

The fog seemed to have thickened still more in the last half hour, and being Sunday as well, there was no traffic nor even a shadowy figure to be seen. But I was in no mood to contemplate the God-forsaken and strangely quiet aspect of the St. Giles Rookery as we took our slow way through the close streets, for I had much to reflect on; and some of the reflections exceedingly curious. Thus I was deep in consideration when Pikestaff edged us grinding round a tight corner, cursed suddenly, and pulled our horses to a sharp halt, bawling 'Give road there.'

Next there was a mutter of conversation addressed to Pikestaff. He replied loudly, 'I'll be buggered if I will,' and my first thought was of no more than a brewer's dray or market wagon blocking us. So far as I could see we were caught in a narrow street, still within St. Giles at some distance yet from Tottenham Court. Such occurrences are commonplace here, these carters being as obstructive as they are surly. But now a shape emerged through the fog to the carriage window. It said politely, 'By your leave, sir,' and opened the door.

I was never so taken aback in my life. The fellow was respectably attired, though muffled up to the eyes, and spoke in the accents of a gentleman. I demanded, 'What the devil?' but was then struck speechless. I had not seen the like since engaged against the highwaymen on Hounslow Heath. It was beyond belief in the heart of London, for I now perceived that he was carrying a cloak over his right arm with the snout of a pistol protruding from it.

'Be damned,' I started again, but he said, 'If you please,' just as polite. 'Pray be good enough to step down.'

'I'll see you to hell,' I announced. 'Why should I?'

'This.' He revealed the pistol ready cocked. 'I trust you'll not force me to use it. But there are those who desire some conversation with you.'

It was a simple choice, for the fellow seemed strangely uneasy, and no person of sensibility argues with a cocked pistol held in an uneasy hand. Moreover in this fog, and the twisting alleys of the rookery close by, he could shoot and vanish in a minute. But no person of sensibility may abduct Jeremy Sturrock so impudently either, and this was as good a way of getting to the heart of the matter as any other. My mind was made up as sharp as my answer. 'Very well,' I said.

'I'm obliged,' he replied. 'Be good enough to walk to the other carriage. Quickly, if you please.'

'I don't propose to loiter,' I assured him, stepping down to the street and taking in the scene. Our own vehicle half round the corner and well jammed; another a few yards ahead. One man holding our horses, one more with a further pistol trained up at Pikestaff, and him sitting as stiff as a block of wood. I fancied that I caught a flicker of his eyes as I looked back at him, but there was no time for exchanges, as our polite gentleman now seemed excessively anxious, and I said, 'Pray be careful with that thing, sir. If you're not used to them they can go off damnation easy, and there's no need to make an opera. I'm just as eager to meet your principals as it seems they are to meet me.'

= 9 =

I KNOW MY London was well as any man—or as well as
it can be known—but we drove with the blinds down
and by so many twists and turns, through clattering
thoroughfares and then quieter streets, that I doubt even
a ship's sailing-master could have told his whereabouts.
It was mostly in silence and confounded tedious before it
was done, though there was one short conversation
which gave me pause for thought.

There was another man in the carriage with our polite
friend, and the pistol remained much in evidence despite
my assurance that I had no slightest intention of attempt-
ing to escape. 'You'd hardly dare fire if I did,' I said to try
their temper, for at this time we were in one of the busy
places and pretty well surrounded by traffic. 'I could step
out here easy,' though I added to myself that it would
have been at the considerable risk of being run down or
trampled under horses.

'Not so, master,' the other answered, making a slight
movement. As fast as I have ever seen it done, a long
knife appeared in his hand, and he grinned at me with a
sort of ferocious amiability; something very different
from the quiet manner of the younger fellow. Thick-set
and beef-faced, rough hair and beard, as strong as an ox
by the look of him and certainly no gentleman; there was
a reddish glint in his eyes under shaggy brows, and I
formed the unpleasant conclusion that he was more than

a little crazed. That, I confess, did cause me some disquiet, for even my wit is of little use against a madman. 'Bide ye quiet, master,' he said, with the same ferocious humor. 'So much as fart and I'll hamstring yer.'

'It would be as well, Mr. Sturrock,' the other man advised. 'My friend here has decided opinions and a quick temper. But pray put that away, Brother Inge,' he begged. 'There's no need of it.'

'So ho,' I observed to myself, 'So I've found Butcher Inge with a damnation vengeance,' while that rascal mopped and grinned at me like a rabid dog. 'Not yet,' he said, and I half expected to see him slavering. 'But there will be. The mighty shall be overthrown, and them as lickspittle to 'em shall be cut down like the corn.'

'Quite so,' I said.

Thereafter fell another and more thoughtful silence during which the murderous monster sat with his arms folded, regarding me with an unwavering stare, grunting and muttering to himself now and again. I was more than thankful when we edged round one more corner, rolled over cobblestones, and stopped at last. From somewhere behind came the groan of heavy gates shutting, and my better-disposed captor opened the carriage door.

So far as I could see, we were within a yard closed on all sides by tall and grimy buildings and, from the taint of mud and sewage in the fog, somewhere close by the river at low tide. But I had no time for careful observation. With Butcher Inge and two more following, the other fellow leading the way, we passed through a narrow entrance, up three flights of dark stairs and what was little more than a ladder with a trap door overhead, and finally to a bare little chamber. Not a stick in it, naked boards and walls, one little opening or sort of doorway that you would have to crawl on your hands and knees to get through, a smaller heavy-framed window, and all stinking of mildew and stale cold.

I looked about with some distaste, and said, 'I trust you don't mean me to lodge here for long.'

'Better'n the condemned cell at Newgate, cully,' observed Inge, who had followed us up, and only got his barrel-chest through the narrow trap with difficulty. 'Where you've sent many a good man before now.'

'If you please, Brother Inge.' The other man seemed to be very near asking my pardon. 'I fear it's poor accommodation, Mr. Sturrock. But you'll understand that I must abide by a decision made in committee.' He looked at Inge. 'We must all abide by it.'

Inge emitted a curious growl, and I demanded, 'What decision?'

He seemed uneasy. 'That will be made clear.'

'Young man,' I announced, 'I've been patient so far, but now let's have an end of this play acting. I refuse to remain in this filthy hole, and I require to know who your principals are.'

'Sir,' he replied, 'I fear you have no choice. And we have no principals. In the eyes of God all men are equals and brothers. For myself I could wish no part of this, but we have set our hands to the plough and there can be no turning back. Thus it is written in the Book of Romans, "As some affirm that we say, Let us do evil that good may come".'

'Dear God,' I thought, 'another preacher,' and Inge started, 'That be buggered,' but the fellow put on a sudden air of command which was anything but equal. 'Brother Inge, pray go down. You know the only task appointed to you here.' He watched the ugly villain edge himself back through the trap, again with a baleful look at me, then finished, 'Inge has a certain duty. He will remain below with the other two, and I beg of you, do not provoke him. He is not a reasonable man.'

'But you are, I fancy.' I had made a blunder. I had expected them to take me to Marylebone, where I might have discovered something, and I had allowed them to bring me to this place instead. It was time to set it right if I could, and I repeated, 'You are a reasonable man, sir, and a reasonable man would tell me why I have been brought here.'

He gazed at me in open astonishment. 'Come, Mr. Sturrock. We are well informed about you. You have been moved from Bow Street to a more secret department. You have been busy about particular enquiries in the last several days. Can you wonder that there are persons who wish to know . . .' he checked himself. 'What you are engaged upon.'

So it was simple enough. They must needs find out how much I knew about them; and my own tale had come back to bedevil me. I could have laughed had I been in a laughing mood. The man was nobody's fool, however, and I went off on another tack. 'Very well, sir. But you are a decent man, and if I'm any judge, you've no stomach for this wicked business. Get yourself out of it while you can. Give me your name and tell me what "Cato" means, and I'll promise that no harm shall come to you in the end.'

'Cato?' he asked. 'You don't know what that is? Then you're harmless.' He stared at me in astonishment again, and then burst out, 'Decent I am, I hope, but also true. And you can promise nothing, for it's you and your like that have driven decent men to these extremities. I shall say no more. There are others who will come to question you.'

'So be it, if you're set on hanging,' I said. 'But when may I expect these others?'

'That I cannot tell you. They have more important affairs presently. But I advise you to pray, as I shall pray for you.'

'One moment,' I demanded, for I could see a hope of working on the fellow's conscience. 'Tell me, do you condone wicked murder? Particularly the murder of Bragg in a manner so unspeakable?'

His look gave away his desperation. 'That was done in haste, and without thought or orders. Before Heaven I condone nothing. But I am one voice among many. God help us,' he added, 'we can only work with the tools He places in our hands.'

He turned away to get down the ladder, and I said, 'You blame God for too much—for my part I have a better opinion of Him,' but there was no answer, only the sound of bolts shot under the trap.

My first thought now was to find a means of escape for when I should have urgent need of it, and to make clear what follows I shall describe my prison with some care. First the trap, which, as I have already said, was bolted from below and of such a meagre size that the thickest Inge could only get through it with difficulty. Next the walls, of old but solid brick and impenetrable without implements. The ceiling sloping down steep to the equally meagre window, small paned and a stout frame; but that would hardly be a graceful exit, as I discovered when I cleared a part of the begrimed glass to peer out and down. For as if to tantalize me, the fog was now clearing a little, and I perceived that this building was exactly on the river, or rather on an evilly glistening stretch of mud and indescribable filth some thirty feet below. Nobody of a nice consideration for his person would choose to leave willingly by that route.

There remained only the small opening in the side wall, and I crawled through that distastefully to find a curious long garret festooned with cobwebs. Sloping rafters and then the roof slates, and some of these loose, for I could see chinks of what little light there was in the darkening February afternoon. Bare boards, nothing which might be used as an implement or weapon, and no other window; but a further gleam of light at the far end, which turned out to be a sort of ventilation aperture, big enough to get my head through though not quite so wide as to admit my shoulders. There was no graceful exit that way, either.

It looked at first that Providence was still unkindly mocking me, yet had I but known it, He was working in His own mysterious ways, etc., for it was by means of this insignificant hole that I later made a fearful discovery. As it appeared now, however, I was merely looking down into the yard by which we had entered, and with little further advantage. The carriage was still here, now turned about and ready to leave, with the gates open, and my friend of the tender though fanatic conscience was standing by it and seemingly giving Inge last instructions. But then I realised that by the peculiar configuration of the place, enclosed by tall buildings all round, very near every word they were saying floated up as clear as the Whispering Gallery of St. Paul's.

'. . . About eight tonight . . . not safe to bring it before utter darkness and pray God the fog comes down again . . . tell you to have the greatest care of it.' Inge gave his mad laugh at that. 'By God we shall, or more like by the Devil—it's his plaything.' A stern rebuke then. 'Do not blaspheme, Brother Inge—we have most need of blessing.'

He turned to the carriage, and Inge said, 'Stay now, Master Blake. When will the others come for him up there?' but I did not catch all the answer. In part it sounded like, '. . . Not before Tuesday . . . business with our committees in other parts of the country before our final meeting . . .' He faced back to Inge, however, and his words became clearer. 'I charge you, treat him kindly.' Inge made some protest, but the other went on sharply, 'He is already condemned by his own actions, but he shall have a fair hearing. He has been known to show mercy in the past when he might have been harsh. See that he has food and drink. Here's money for it.'

Something then changed hands, and he got into the carriage. Inge closed and barred the gates, came back to the building and passed out of my sight, and I drew a long breath and observed, 'So ho.'

It was now near four o'clock, the light closing fast, and I returned to the other chamber with more to reflect on. First: That only one man could have murdered Bragg without orders, and then contrived the ambush and my own capture. Second: Blake's remark that the conspirators were well informed about me, and Clancy's word of treachery to Mrs. Clancy. Third: That by this time Maggsy and Jagger would know of the abduction, for Pikestaff must and would report on it, but unless they had come upon some fresh information themselves what could they do? From the direction of our investigations so far their thoughts would turn to The Hog In The Pound and Marylebone, nor could or would Pikestaff tell them any better; and that, perhaps, was just as well. A style of rescue mounted by Master Maggsy with Jagger in fighting mood was the last thing I wanted. The contemplation of it made my blood run cold.

For I dare not attempt escape yet. It would be damned uncomfortable, and just as dangerous, but I must lie quiet, seemingly a hapless prisoner. So long as I remained here these villains would feel secure, but alarm them in any way and they would scatter; we might take a few of the underlings, but the ringleaders would vanish. Moreover I had already learned something, and I meant to learn more; not least what it was that would be brought with such care and secrecy about eight o'clock tonight.

Therefore I must work with subterfuge, which required observation and time. And the last was a com-

modity which I had in plenty according to Mr. Blake. If
the principals in this monstrous business were to be
about their arrangements in the country tomorrow, and
he did not expect them to come to question me before
Tuesday, there must at least be two conclusions. The
first that their conspiracy was more widespread than
even I had supposed—and all the more reason to scotch it
once and for all. The other, that in their own cant the
clock was not set to strike yet, perhaps not for several
more days. And before then I might spring my own
surprises.

There were several church clocks which rang the slow
passing hours, and one from its chimes without doubt
was St. Paul's, from which I concluded that I must be
somewhere in the maze of wharves east of Blackfriar's
Bridge. A useful discovery, but not so important as
knowing the time of day, for it was now too dark to see
my watch. I counted six before the trap was unbolted
and pushed up a few inches in a glimmer of light from
below. Inge was down there, for I heard him muttering,
but saw nothing except a mug and tin platter pushed
onto the floor without a word spoken. Then I was left in
the dark again, to extract what comfort I could from a
vile and greasy mutton pie and a pot of thin small beer.
    Another leaden hour passed by, damnably cold, while
I watched a few dim lanterns on the river. The butcher
and his men now seemed to be in the lower part of the
building, for there was no further sound, and at last I
groped my way quietly through the long garret to my
observation post above the yard. The fog now thinned to
a light mist, as silent as the grave and no movement yet,
but a faint glow of light across the cobbles below.
    It seemed a long eternity, the church clocks chiming
again, before I heard the jangle of a bell—two short pulls
and two long. One fellow appeared, crossing the yard to

the gates to swing them open, while Inge and the other came after him carrying lanterns. Next a common tradesman's van drawn by a dejected looking horse; and even before that backed round I knew what it was, and where it had come from. There was no mistaking the squeak and the dab-footed gait of the miserable animal. 'So ho,' I breathed. 'Watkins' yard again.'

The carter was as surly as all the rest of his tribe. He said, 'Get this bleedin' lot off quick and let me be done with it—I don't fancy that sort of load.' I wondered for an instant whether we should see another corpse brought out; even Master Maggsy or Jagger. It was a mysterious spectacle in the mist and wavering light: the squat figure of Inge and the other two rascals casting uncertain shadows, the ungainly horse as bony as a skeleton, the carter with a sack folded over his head and shoulders like an unholy monk. 'I hope to God none of 'em's leaking,' he said, and Inge replied madly 'We'll all get our arses singed if they are.'

'What the devil is it?' I asked myself, as Inge lifted out what was plainly a small barrel or firkin. 'Surely nothing so commonplace as smuggling?' Then the carter cried, 'Keep them bloody lights well away!' and I caught sight of the red markings. It dawned on me as sudden as if the thing had exploded in front of my eyes. They were taking off a load of gunpowder.

I counted four fourteen-pound kegs carried out of my sight and into the building. Half a hundredweight altogether. More than enough to cause a fearful destruction.

There was no need to wonder what they meant to do with that deadly load. It was certainly not innocent duck-shooting. Nor was it intended merely to assassinate one man alone, for there was enough powder here to blow down half a street. But I could see now what Bragg's part had been, and why he had been so brutally silenced. As a one-time lower servant in Lord Harrowby's household and a malcontent, he had been the very man they had need of to advise them where to place the explosive in or below his lordship's residence, most likely by way of some little known entrance to the cellars. Moreover, since they were keeping the stuff as close handy as this, only on the edge of the city, it must be the residence in Grosvenor Square.

Bragg's murder made it certain that the conspiracy was aimed at Harrowby. But to what end if, as Abel Makepenny declared, he was of no particular importance despite his high-sounding office? Ponder as I might, I could see no answer to that question yet, and until it was answered I saw no reason to amend my present strategy.

So long as the powder remained safely in this old warehouse, the clock was not set to strike. It was harmless enough while it remained here; or so I hoped, for sitting several floors above a magazine with a madman like Inge at large was not the most convenient of situations. When the rascals showed signs of moving it, I might have to move quickly myself, but until that moment I must compose myself to wait and watch while devising my own plans. And, had I but known it, Master Maggsy and Jagger were already busy about theirs.

Unshaven and unwashed, reduced to the most disgusting shifts for the simplest necessities of nature, I shall draw a discreet veil over the hours and days that followed. The trap was only opened to push in the poor muck which passed for food and drink. Nothing was said at these times, for plainly none of the rascals was all that anxious to come too close to me, although I heard them about below. Once or twice Inge came and bawled rude enquiries, which I answered in tones of despondency, and on one occasion even asked what he would take to allow me to escape. I promised him very near everything, but I shall not repeat what he replied.

I slept as well as I could for the cold through the hours of darkness, and otherwise passed much of my time at my spyhole observing the yard, though there was little to see. On Monday morning Inge went out early and came back about noon. One of the others then left, and when this fellow returned he brought a small surprise, though by no means pleasurable. Of all horrible creatures, he was accompanied by that wicked torch boy who had lured me into the ambush on Saturday. The little wretch appeared to be on the best of terms, laughing and chattering like a magpie down there; seemingly, they were employing him to run errands, for he went out and came back several times, and I fancy that he even brought in my unsavory victuals.

So that day passed, darkness falling early and the fog closing down again. I watched from my observation post until the church clocks struck midnight, but there was no sign of moving the gunpowder. The light at last vanished in the yard below, and I settled myself to uneasy sleep with several somewhat unusual prayers. For tomorrow I was to be 'questioned'—a damned impudence, as it were me on trial—and I should have need of my wits about me.

My unusual prayers merged into phantasmagoric dreams in which I was fighting Butcher Inge for possession of a monstrous meat cleaver while that horrid boy danced around a stack of powder kegs brandishing a torch and flinging sparks everywhere. So real it was that I found myself suddenly half awake and indeed grappling with something unseen that seemed to fight like a wildcat, whispering wicked curses. My first thought was that Inge had taken leave of what little was left of his senses, but a voice then snarled in the dark, 'God's sake, go easy, will yer?'

'What the devil?' I demanded, now perceiving that I was doing my best to strangle a smaller and lighter dimly-seen figure. 'Who's that?'

'Alfred,' it hissed. 'God's sake, lay off and keep quiet. You knows me. You see me t'other day. Wif a torch.'

That confounded torch boy, and by no means a dream. 'You?' I started. 'Is this a fresh trick? What d'you want, and how in damnation did you get here?' I took a fresh grip of him, and he repeated 'Lay off. I come across the roof. There's a flight of steps next door if you knows where to look. Your two coves sent me to fetch you out, and a right pair of bleeders they are as well. They're down below.'

'There's explanation needed here,' I said, but he answered, 'Ain't no time. They catched me by Watkins' Yard, that's all; and the big'n found this place, which I knows of anyway. I knows everywhere about these parts. It's Broken Wharf, close by Blackfriars.' He stopped for breath and produced a folded paper. 'The other says I was to give you this. And he says you'd give me a sov'rin. So let's have it and get out of here quick. If them coves down below catches me I dunno what they'll do to you, but they'll cut my throat for certain.'

'Be quiet a minute,' I said, for this required consideration; not least whether I could trust the little villain. That was easy answered, however. I had little choice. Further explanations also could wait, and the rest was a matter of my own strategy. I turned over several plans in my mind, while the boy muttered with impatience beside me, and then I announced, 'There we have it,' and fumbled for my purse to feel out a sovereign, which he clutched at in the dark like a starving jackdaw. It went to my heart, but I continued, 'That's your first, and there'll be another at least if you do what you're told. So listen carefully. Tell Maggsy there are reasons why I can't leave here tonight. He and Jagger are to keep quiet and out of sight tomorrow, but he must inform Abel Makepenny that all my conclusions are correct. D'you understand?'

'I ain't a fool. All your conclusions is correct,' he repeated, and I went on, 'Now, you must all come back at this same time tomorrow night. Maggsy and Jagger are to fetch my carriage and leave it close but out of sight. Maggsy is to wait there, but you must bring Jagger up here with you.' I thought it best not to explain what I wanted Jagger for. 'Is that understood also?' He nodded again, and I added as an afterthought, 'Tell Jagger to bring my pistols with him.'

'Pistols, is it?' he whispered. 'Which of 'em are you going to shoot?'

'None of your business,' I told him. 'Be off now. God knows what my two rascals down there might do if they have to wait too long.'

'And thankful to go,' he answered pertly, crawling away through the opening in the garret.

By the time I had followed him, he was already hoisting himself through a hole in the roof, where it appeared that he had removed a number of the loose slates. 'And don't forget the other sov'rin neither,' he enjoined me as he vanished.

After that there was a faint scrabbling above my head and then silence. I was left with the paper he had given me, which seemed like several letters folded together, and which by a further perversity of Fate I could not read until daylight.'

It came damnably slow. Another eternity before I could make out that the packet contained a brief scrawl from Maggsy enclosing two other sealed sheets, the first in Abel Makepenny's clerkly hand, and the second in an unfamiliar writing addressed to me at Soho Square.

There is no need to repeat Maggsy's few lines, but here is what Abel said.

'Re: Ld. Harrowby as follows; and an unconscionable affair I had procuring it. Monday to Windsor for Audience of His Majesty. Remains there the night, returns Tuesday to meeting P. Council St. James Pal. Wednesday to dine with Count and Countess Lieven, Wimbledon. Thursday Ld. Liverpool and Ministers to sup with him at residence G. Sq. Friday to country seat . . . Myself am much engaged at Bow St. as there are requests to send men to Nth re:increasing disorder there, but I await word from you. This failing by Tuesday shall place your conclusions, etc., before the Magistrate, tho' what G.A. may make of them who can say. I incline myself that you are making a great business out of a few mere crackpots, tho' it is said that affairs in the Nth aforementioned are serious . . .'

'Am I, by God?' I demanded. 'Be damned to the North; the main mischief's here.' For there it was plain. The Prime Minister and his Cabinet to sup at Grosvenor Square on Thursday, and half a hundredweight of gunpowder waiting for 'em. There was Harrowby's importance now made clear—pretty well the entire government, or such of it as mattered most, all together under his roof—and in the present state of the country the explosion itself might be the signal for a general uprising and all its direful consequences. 'But for me,' I said. But was careful to add, 'And the Grace of God.'

Which same Grace was evident in the second letter, for of all persons it was from Mr. Gladwick Mannering, the other somewhat Radical American gentleman with whom it will be remembered I had exchanged views at Lady's Dorothea's residence. I shall not set down the whole of it, as my publisher is already counting the pages, and Mr. Mannering clearly enjoyed writing at some length with an elegant literary distinction, as I do also. He started, 'I am advised to address myself to you, Sir, by our mutually respected hostess Lady Dorothea Hookham-Dashwood, since I am much concerned that some mishap must have befallen my friend and compatriot, Mr. Edward Lampeter . . .'

'So ho,' I observed. Mr. Lampeter, it seemed, had appointed to meet Mr. Mannering at The Orange Tree Coffee House on Friday last, but had not appeared. Enquiry at his lodging had then revealed that he had not been seen since Thursday morning, though his baggage, etc., was still there. Nor had further enquiries disclosed anything more, but he had lately been invited to a committee with whose views he expressed much sympathy and interest, having . . . most decided opinions himself, and coming of a Boston family which had suffered much in the late Wars of Independence . . .'

And here we came to the nub of it. 'Nor do I abate my own thoughts on these matters, but Mr. Lampeter was becoming exceedingly uneasy at certain intentions of these persons, who wished to recruit him to their cause. What these intentions are he did not wholly confide to me, but he had attended several secret meetings at a loft in Cato Street, in the district of Marylebone . . .'

'There, by God, we have it at last,' I said. 'Cato *Street*. There is my answer.'

— 10 —

It may be imagined with what impatience I waited through that never-ending Tuesday. I shall confess even to some little anxiety, for though I have learned to live with danger, and meet it with my wits, I had no doubt of my fate if I made only one trifling error now.

As before I passed most of the day at my spyhole. Inge went out early and a fresh man came in, by the look of him merely another underling. He was followed soon after by the torch boy, Alfred, seemingly still running errands, and him I watched carefully lest he should show any sign of betraying me. But all remained quiet. My poor food was passed through the trap, again with no closer approach and no word spoken; the morning passed into afternoon, and it was very near dark before the gates were opened to admit the carriage. 'And this will decide it,' I said, expecting to see two or three or more of their precious committee appear. But to my surprise only Mr. Blake got out. And that was a fair omen, I thought. I fancied I had the measure of that gentleman.

He seemed in haste, exchanging only a few words as he hurried into the building, and I barely had time to get back to the trap before he pushed it up and came through. Not only in haste but also uneasy, and for a minute I feared that I could smell betrayal in the air, or else that something had gone amiss, perhaps that the villains had been warned and had changed their plans.

Either way it meant short shrift for me, but I had already decided on my defence, and I put on a nice tone of half puzzlement and half anger before he had time to speak himself. 'Come, sir, this is a poor way to treat a man who's more than half inclined to your way of thinking. I'd expected some of your committee so that I could explain myself. How long must I wait for them?'

He had brought a lantern, which he set down on the floor between us. 'They have great matters to attend to, and neither do I have much time. I will be open with you, Mr. Sturrock. I beg of you, as you hope for salvation, speak the truth and speak it briefly. What do you know of our intentions? And how are you disposed toward them?'

I was right about the man. These God-bothering radicals are forever eager for converts to bolster up their own doubts, and I saw no harm in presenting him with one. 'As to the first, nothing but rumours, which it's been my duty to investigate. You may not be aware of it, but there are many labouring people who know there's something afoot, though none of 'em can say just what it is. I'm bound to do my duty, sir, whatever my private thoughts may be. But as to those I'll tell you plain. In my opinion the time is more than ripe for change. I see empty bellies and unemployment all about, and I don't like it any more than you do.' In which I was speaking the truth.

'I hope I may believe you. If I may, let us both thank God.' He seemed about to offer up a prayer, but went on as if half to himself, 'We must needs work with the tools that the Lord places to our hands. I said I'd be open with you, Mr. Sturrock, and I will. There is to be a meeting of our full Council tomorrow night, and your own fate might well hang on what I have to report there.'

The conspiratorial cant once more, though the poor fellow had no notion of how much he was giving away. I said, 'Then I hope it will be a good one, for I can be of service to you. In my turn I can report that there's nothing in these rumours.'

He looked at me sadly. 'You would be lying. Moreover, it will all be done by then, and fearful work it will be. Inge will oppose me,' he continued, again half to himself. 'But I wish you well. Shall I tell you why? Do you recollect a young woman who was once known as Polly Andrews?'

I affected to cast my mind back. 'Why, yes. Brussels, after Waterloo, some five years past. A matter of abduction and several other capital charges. But as I remember, I considered that she had been lead astray by bad company.'

He nodded. 'You showed mercy. And I have reason to be grateful for it.'

Even in that light I could see a flush on his cheek, and I thought, 'God help him, he's taken a fancy to the woman.' And how inscrutable are the ways of Providence, that a mere whim to save her neck five years since might now save my own. 'We must all be merciful when we can,' I observed.

'We must indeed. And to him who shows mercy, mercy shall be shown.' He looked around the place distastefully. 'I fear there is little I can do to ameliorate your condition. Inge is in charge here, and I beg you again, do not provoke him. But I shall leave you the lantern.'

With that he got himself back through the trap and shot the bolts beneath it once more, while I said softly, 'And I'll save your neck as well if I can, for you're a good man in your own way. But I'll have all the rest—all of 'em together in one basket tomorrow night at Cato Street.'

There was still the danger that Inge might take a

bloodthirsty fit, or that the boy would play us false yet; and I doubted that Jagger would much like the part I had cast for him. But there was nothing more I could do except count the creeping hours. The church bells struck midnight, and one, and then two, and I was very near fearing that my plans had indeed gone awry before I heard a soft whistle of a stave of *Lilliburlero*.

The urchin appeared suddenly like an ugly dwarf, and a minute later Jagger plunged through the roof after him with a clatter of slates which made my blood run cold. 'God's sake, quiet!' I hissed at him, and we all three lay as still as mice, with Jagger muttering under his breath and the boy whispering, 'If they heard that, they won't reckon it's cats, and if they come up I'm hopping off quick, they'd have my bowels out for this.'

It seemed like another hour, but there was no alarm from below, and at last I murmured, 'Very good. Be ready to lead the way, boy. Did you bring the pistols?' I asked Jagger, to break it to him easy. 'You might need 'em. You're staying here.'

That stopped his muttering like a cannonball. 'I'm what?' he demanded. 'Not bloody likely I ain't. If it wasn't for me you'd still be here yourself.'

There was no time to listen to him, for the rascal was as bad as Maggsy in one of his obstinate fits. I very near despaired of hammering the necessity of it into his head. 'All you must do is move about and talk to yourself a bit so they can hear you and think I'm still safe. There's only three of 'em and they never venture this far. If they do, you've got the pistols.' Though I could only pray that he wouldn't have to use them. But that was a considered danger, and I finished. 'Be damned, I thought you was a sportsman.'

The good fellow saw his duty in the end, and we left him with a sick-spaniel look for the precarious journey that followed. That is another veil I shall draw. To this day I do not know which was worse: the foggy darkness, wet slates, and fearful slopes, the river seemingly a mile below; or that horrible boy's admonitions and curses in between whistling snatches of *Lilliburlero* through his teeth. At one extremity I could swear that he was clutching me by the hair while my legs dandled over nothingness, at the next he had me by an ankle as I gazed down at another black abyss. Astride a ridge, crawling round a tottering chimney stack, sliding on my backside towards a further precipice, a flight of wooden steps, shaking and half rotten. Then God's good solid earth beneath our feet, and a quick passage by devious ways to the alley in which Maggsy was waiting with the chaise.

Much must be passed over again, notably Master Maggsy's observations when he learned that Jagger was left behind, and the manner in which he drove us back to Soho Square himself. We took the boy with us—for we dare not let him loose now, and I had other uses for him yet—and even he was shocked into silence.

But there must be some explanations, and Maggsy gave the gist of them while I was cleaning myself, shaving, and eating. 'Nice thing leaving Jaggs there, when it was him found out where you was,' he said spitefully. 'He has his wits sometimes, and you know how he can get stablehands to talk. Well, he went to Watkins' Yard, like you said, and got the cove there and filled him up with God knows how much beer, it being Sunday. Couldn't find out much about Limping Mick, but . . .'

'I'm pretty certain who killed Limping Mick and Bragg,' I interjected. 'I'll deal with that later. Keep to finding me.'

'Jaggs discovered that van was hired for a particular special job on Sunday night. Then when we come back here, me from Portman Square, Pikestaff was waiting for us, and he said what had happened to you, and also there wasn't no need to go looking for Sergeant Clancy any more, as he'd come back as well. Which seemed what you reckoned anyway, so I says to Jaggs, "Now we've got to start looking for Sturrock, instead," but couldn't think of anywhere else but The Hog In The Pound and Marylebone. I said if we go anywhere near The Hog again there'll be murder done, and very like has been already, and Jaggs says for want of anything better why don't we follow the van that night. Which we done easy enough, as it was going uncommon careful in the fog, and so we come to Broken Wharf. Where we catched him ferreting about.' He jerked his head at the boy, who was now busy stuffing Melton Pie into his mouth as fast as he could go.

'Which it seems he's well acquainted with these villains, as he does jobs for 'em now and again, and we told him what we'd do to him. So he found out they'd got somebody up at the top of that old warehouse, and he says he knows of a way across the roofs.'

'That's right,' said the boy, with a strange sort of admiration for Maggsy. 'They offered I could please myself whether they had my bowels out, if I didn't hang first, or you'd give me a sov'rin. Which I chose the sov'rin. And you promised me another.'

'You shall have it,' I told him, though it was a reckless extravagance. 'But I've other work for you first. Is there anything more?' I asked Maggsy.

'Portman Square,' he started, but I said, 'We can dispense with that. It's of no further interest. The woman once known as Polly Andrews was or is lodging down there, with a man named Blake, who's most probably a dissenting minister. They're the means by which Mr. Lampeter was introduced to the gang, and that's all we need say about 'em. What of Clancy and his men? Did you tell any of them that you'd found me, or how you meant to effect my escape?'

'Know it all before I open my mouth, don't you?' he enquired bitterly. 'But we ain't seen hide nor hair of the Clancy lot since Sunday, so couldn't tell 'em anything. Nor wouldn't, anyway.'

'And my message to Abel Makepenny? You took that?'

He nodded. 'First thing this morning. Abel said he'd put it before the Beak, though couldn't reckon what the upshot'd be, as he's took a nasty spite against you and ain't likely to believe a word you say.'

'He will before I've finished with him,' I pronounced. 'Very good, then. You've done pretty well, all things considered. So now we'll snatch a few hours rest. We've a busy day before us. And first,' I said with rich anticipation, 'an early visit to Bow Street.'

In all the tribulations of that dangerous affair, my conversation with our Lord Jackass of a Magistrate remains the one pure pleasure, though conducted with the utmost politeness—at least on my side. I took the boy with me for certain reasons, and when we entered Abel Makepenny's office that excellent old man was in a fine fit of flusters. 'What the demnition have you been up to, Jer'my?' he begged. 'And what's the tale your Maggsy was telling me? Be demned, I don't more'n half believe it myself.' He lowered his voice and nodded towards the inner door. 'Nor he won't have any of it. He declares it's all a waggonload of poppycock.'

'Then we must persuade him, and do it quick,' I said. 'I shall want you as a witness, Abel. We need this creature also.'

Not waiting any further, I knocked on the door and entered with Abel and the boy behind, now perceiving that our Magistrate had been hard at the Port again, for he regarded me considerably bloodshot. He gazed from me to the boy, and demanded, 'What in the name of God is that? And what do you want here?'

'To lay information, sir,' I replied. 'A matter of half a hundredweight of gunpowder, to be conveyed secretly into the cellars of Lord Harrowby's residence. This to mark the occasion of his lordship entertaining the Prime Minister and Cabinet at supper tomorrow. Together with knowledge of a meeting of the conspirators concerned tonight. I believe Mr. Makepenny had already apprised you of my investigations.'

'Aye, he has.' He continued to regard me bloodshot. 'It's a tarradiddle of damned nonsense that you've made up to serve some purpose of your own. Or you're cracked.'

'Why, no, sir,' I said modestly. 'Not that I've noticed. Though one of these aforesaid conspirators may be. A murderous rascal by the name of Inge.'

And then the boy must need pipe up. 'That's right.' He addressed himself to the Magistrate, not the least abashed by the August Presence. 'That's Butcher Inge, and he's got a sack for the heads. He's going to cut 'em all off and have 'em stuck on spikes on Tower Hill.'

'Be quiet.' I could have wished the wretch anywhere, for this indeed sounded a note of madness. 'One of the ringleaders, if not the head of them, is Arthur Thistlewood,' I continued quickly. 'You'll recollect his part in the St. Peter's Fields affair in Manchester last year.'

The name of Thistlewood gave him pause for thought, but he remained gazing horribly at the urchin. 'A sack? To put their heads in? God help us, we're beset by Bedlam,' he cried. 'And Thistlewood's mere wind and piss. Get shot of 'em both, Makepenny, or I'll have 'em arrested.'

Poor Abel did not know which way to look, but I now produced my ace of trumps—several carefully sealed up papers on which I had been at work since seven o'clock that morning. 'Sir,' I said, 'I have here a full report of the conspiracy. To the effect that these dangerous Radicals mean to destroy our present elected Government, bring about a general uprising, and thereafter set up a caucus of their own. I am hereby formally requesting you to place a force at my disposal to put a stop to it. And Mr. Makepenny is my witness.'

'Poppycock,' he announced rudely, but I said, 'Very good, sir. If it is there's no harm done. But if you refuse your men, I shall take this account to *The Times* newspaper office. I am sufficiently well known at Printing House Square to have them pay attention to me. And I say again that Mr. Makepenny is my witness.'

For several minutes I was concerned for the gentleman's health. His face assumed a strangely purple look, but before he could gather breath enough to whisper, I added, 'You'll take my meaning, sir. If there's no explosion I shall be the fool. But if there is . . .' I paused and considered him kindly. 'You will be in a very curious situation.'

You could have heard a flea sneeze in that office. 'Whereas if you see fit to instruct Mr. Makepenny and me to make our arrangements, as we always used to do to everybody's satisfaction in the time of our previous Magistrate, you need not concern yourself further. For my part I want nothing out of this,' I finished. 'Merely the accomplishment of my duty. But for you, sir, I fancy the Government and even His Majesty would prove singularly appreciative.'

It was as good as done then. The gentleman made a number of reflections of a remarkably personal nature, but at last he cried, 'Do as you think fit, Makepenny, but for God's sake get this rascal out of my sight.'

The rest was dispositions, although I did not disguise from myself that much might yet be touch and go. Abel found me twelve men, all armed, and the best of our forces in London. Three of these and the boy I despatched to Broken Wharf, where they were to loiter about as labouring persons while the boy went in and out on errands, as was his habit; and I made it abundantly clear what would happen to him if he failed us. He was to report the first sign of danger to Jagger or other alarm, in which event our men were to go in immediately and arrest everybody there. Otherwise, they were to wait until Inge came out—for I was certain that he must attend the meeting—before making their entry.

Two others I had mounted, one attached to the wharf party and the other with my own, these to act as fast messengers. Then, consulting Horwood's map of London, we studied the area of Cato Street, discovering it to be a minor *cul-de-sac* off Crawford Place, and two more men were sent there for a preliminary reconnaissance. The others were to wait at The Cricket Club Tavern, which was conveniently close in the Edgware Road, and which I proposed to make my command post, with Maggsy for liaison. And finally I arranged for suitable conveyances to be held nearby for our expected prisoners.

By three o'clock our men had marked the loft, and I ordered my own rider to Broken Wharf to report our position and send the other back. This one came at four with the information that all was still quiet there. By five it was getting dark and foggy again, with no movement yet, and I began to feel uneasy. But at six my first messenger returned with word that Inge had left the warehouse; and soon after this, Maggsy reported that a light had been put on in the loft, and that persons heavily muffled were now entering after giving a signal knock at the street door.

And next Clancy entered the tavern. By this time there was a fair crowd present, labourers, tradesmen, etc., and he did not see me at first, although he was looking about narrowly; then Maggsy followed him and the two came face to face. Maggsy glanced across at me, and Clancy followed his look; I pushed through to them fast, and we both spoke together. He: 'God be praised.' Me: 'Clancy, I want explanations, and I want 'em quick. Where have you been these last days, and what're you here after now?'

'Seeking for this place,' the impudent rogue replied. 'And laying out of sight the better to find it. What else does a dacint man do whin he finds he's got a traitor in his own company?'

'It's what I do that matters,' I retorted. 'And I mean to see him hang.'

'Aye,' Clancy said, 'well maybe.' But Maggsy put in, 'You won't hang nobody if you don't set about it quick. The latest word is that they're all met now. Ain't nobody else gone in, and the last was your man, Inge.'

'Near enough a score,' our Bow Street man murmured, now concealed with all the others of his force in the darkness of an entryway. 'That door next to the butcher's shop. Three quick double knocks, then two more. They say something before it's opened to 'em.'

'The password and countersign,' I observed, surveying the scene. A few dim gleams of light in the fog, a woman's voice raised querulously then falling again, but otherwise all dark, empty, and silent. 'Quick and easy as may be, but if it comes to shooting, try only to wing 'em,' I said, and gave my final orders; though I still less than half trusted Clancy and his rascals. They were best out of the way, but he was plainly determined to attach himself, and I finished, 'Sergeant Clancy, I'll have you seal the open end of the street.'

On that I took the lead, crossed over to the door, and knocked the required signal. There was no answer for a minute, and I half feared we might have to break in before a voice whispered, 'Who's there? Ain't nobody else to come.' I replied, 'A message for Mr. Thistle-wood—from the North and most urgent. Ask the password, will you?' I demanded. 'When does the clock strike?'

'I dunno,' the blockhead muttered. 'That ain't right. It's been changed.' I damned the unlucky chance, but then answered, 'Nobody informed me. I've been on the road two days. Listen for God's sake, there're Bow Street men not far behind, and if they come up with me they'll find all of us.'

The truth never fails the righteous, for there was a startled curse and the door opened at once. Then it was all over in an instant. I moved aside quick; two of our men slipped past me like shadows. A hand over the fellow's mouth, an arm around his neck, and he was brought out bodily without so much as a cough—barely a sound of any sort except the clink and snap of mana-cles.

I cocked my pistols and went in first. Before me now was a flight of loft steps to a half floor, a strong light up there, and the voice of a practised speaker addressing the company. You could hear every word. '*Delenda est Car-thago*, and tomorrow, brothers, Carthage *shall* be de-stroyed. The clock strikes at nine. We are assured that the explosion will be heard in Old Palace Yard, and with its signal I shall lead our march on the House of Com-mons. At that time also Brother Hunt will make his announcement to the City from the Mansion House steps.'

'Take note for the trial,' I whispered to my men behind. 'That's Thistlewood for certain.' While the other, I thought, was undoubtedly the firebrand known as 'Orator Hunt.'

'There cannot be any resistance,' Thistlewood was continuing. 'Our stroke will be too sudden. We shall enter the Chamber, remove the Mace as Cromwell did before us, and I shall read our Declaration of a Provisional Government. Beyond that I have little more to say to you. We must now go into committee to receive reports, and instruct our messengers for Birminghan, Manchester, and other parts. But I will first call on Brother Blake to offer up a prayer for blessing on our enterprise.'

Blake's answer was quiet. 'It would be a blasphemy. I would sooner ask forgiveness for the fearful things we must do.' Inge's voice broke in roughly then. 'It's their heads or ours now. For my part I mean to see theirs on Tower Hill. Aye, and I've got my little sack ready for 'em.'

There was laughter at that, though some disapproval as well, but Thistlewood cried, 'Order if you please, and remember, Brother Inge, ours is the sword of necessity, not mere bloody revenge.'

Revolutionaries the world over, I reflected, forever uttering noble sentiments while inciting others to mischief. I had heard enough, and I took a last glance over my men behind. They were all ready, Master Maggsy well in the rear, and now Clancy looking up at me, flatly disobeying my orders. But there was no way of ordering him out without disclosing our presence, and surprise was our prime necessity. I damned the rascal to Hell, and then advanced up the last few steps. 'Stand as you are,' I said, catching the entire assembly in an instant of silence. 'You're all under arrest. This place is surrounded, and the street sealed off with a hundred men.'

It might still have been done peaceful had it not been for that demented butcher. They were struck like statues, all eyes turned on me, a crowd of fearful faces and gaping mouths, although I could not see the man I most wanted. Thistlewood held in the middle of a word, Blake as if the Lord Himself had struck him, Inge with

the look of a maniac. It was he who started the blood-
shed. He bawled, 'Betrayed—and I know who by,' and
flung himself on Blake. I caught the flash of a knife, and
cried, 'Hold there!' but it was too late. Blake fell with a
terrible cry before I could get to him; Thistlewood and
several others drew pistols. One yelled, 'let 'em not take
us alive!' and six or seven shots crashed so close together
that nobody could say who started the shooting.

In that close space the din, flashes, smoke, and dust
were hellish; the confusion beyond even my pen to
describe. I can only set down what brief glimpses I
caught while engaged myself. Thistlewood bravely encouraging his rascals from behind. A shot taking off my
hat, me firing in the air for fear of hitting our own men.
Clancy thrusting past me with a pistol in his hand. Inge
defying three of our fellows over Blake's body with his
long knife, one of them falling from a wicked upward
thrust, and then myself striking down the madman. I
have never known anything more desperate, and it was a
costly affair before the end. Blake and one of our own
men stabbed to death, half a dozen more on both sides
wounded, and the man I had been looking for killed by a
pistol shot. I caught Clancy looking down at his Corporal
with the weapon still hot, and if such a thing were
possible for him I could have sworn there were tears in
his eyes. But it might have been the smoke and dust
hanging in the air, and I said, 'You've much to explain,
Sergeant Clancy.'

It was an hour later, in the tavern again, Jagger
brought back to us, inclined to regard himself a hero, and
Master Maggsy encouraging him. We had left the Bow
Street men to carry their prisoners into custody, and
now I meant to settle with Clancy even though there
might be little profit in it. I said, 'It was a neat shot in
that confusion. And I can see you had your own reasons.

It wouldn't have done you or Mrs. Clancy's elegant establishment a lot of good if he'd been brought to trial with the rest.'

He looked at me strangely. 'Aye, maybe that. And maybe more than that. Lave it be, Mr. Sturrock. I'm sick to the bowels of it.'

I nodded. 'I can see that as well. You've been fishing in waters too deep for you. But I like to have all things clear, so tell me this. What happened last Thursday night. Were you or Pikestaff in that business?'

'Believe it as you plase,' he replied, 'but I was not. Beyont that I'm not just sure what happened. Nor I doubt anybody iver will be now, except it was Inge that killed Mr. Lampeter, so the Corp'ral told Mrs. Clancy at last. It seems Inge was forever watchful of the poor gentleman, though Thistlewood and the others was after his recruitment, as they considered he might bring opinion in America to their side after it was all done.'

I regarded him unfavourably. 'When did he tell Mrs. Clancy this?'

'Not before it was too late. He came to Panton Street on Sunday night, despairing drunk and cursing himself and ivrybody else, and Mrs. Clancy had it out of him. She's a powerful woman whin she sets about a man. He was under Inge's orders, God help him. But the end of it was that he took himself off out of the house, and me and the boys was seeking him iver since.'

'It's a damned lame tale,' I observed. 'Why did you not suspect him before?'

'It's the best you're iver likely to get,' he retorted. 'If it comes to that, whin did you get to suspicion him yerself?'

'I'll tell you plain,' I said, 'I suspected you more. You had him and your other fellows forever on my heels to find out what I discovered. But apart from Mrs. Clancy he was the only one who knew that I meant to question

Limping Mick. On top of that the murder of Bragg, and the horses said to be restive when they was as quiet as mice, because he daren't come into the mortuary lest by some chance Jonah Gotobed should recognize him. And then my own abduction. Only he could have set that trap and driven me into it so neat. But why, Clancy?' I demanded. 'Why should he have turned that way?' 'He had a great bitterness in him,' Clancy answered soberly. 'He had a brother killed in the Peterloo troubles last year. But I'll be damned if I'd have seen him hanged, or worse, with Inge and the rest of 'em. Lave it be, Mr. Sturrock,' he repeated. 'Save for you and me, who's to say what he was doing at that meeting? Lave it to be thought that he was there on the right side, and let me and Mrs. Sergeant Clancy give him a dacint funeral as befits one of Wellington's old soldiers.'

After that what more could I say?

So Corporal Pikestaff received an old soldier's funeral, which I attended myself out of compliment to Mrs. Clancy; and I was immeasurably pleased that the good lady also contrived to have prayers offered for Mr. Lampeter, as an 'unknown benefactor.' My own most difficult task lay in communicating with Mr. Gladwick Mannering without causing distress, for I could scarcely tell him in precise terms what had befallen his friend. In the end I turned again to the truth, but not too much of it. That Mr. Lampeter's warning had indeed foiled the plot; and most sincerely we all had reason to be profoundly grateful to him; but just as profoundly regretting that I could not add any further information, as the gentleman had come to my chambers without disclosing his identity, and had left again without intimation of his further intentions.

For the rest, the woman Polly Andrews, or Letitia Merritt, or Julia Bracegirdle, vanished once more—no doubt to work more mischief elsewhere—and I was somewhat grieved about Mr. Blake. But he was too deep in the business to have had much hope of escape even with my assistance, and at least he was spared the indignities which awaited his fellow conspirators.

There we have the complete tale of The Cato Street Conspiracy. The curious may read other versions of it if they wish, for the newspapers made a great to do in the last days of February 1820, and you may believe what pleases you best. My part in the affair was not mentioned. It was said that the plot was disclosed by "an informer," which was near enough the truth, and though Master Maggsy and Jagger waxed exceedingly indignant, I am of a more philosophical mind. It has entertained me to set down this account, as I hope it may entertain my admiring readers. As Mr. Wordsworth has observed at some considerable length, a man must regard duty as its own reward, and I shall say no more.

If you have enjoyed this mystery and would like to receive details of other Walker mysteries, please write to:

Mystery Editor
Walker and Company
720 Fifth Avenue
New York, New York 10019